IN A LOST WORLD

The seven Kindred Shoni Tribes are of a race who love the earth. They are a copper-skinned people, surviving wild cousins of the tamed American red man, who dwell beyond the shoulders of the earth, within the Arctic Circle, in a volcano-warmed land which they call Nato'wa.

The Shoni tribesmen have good cause to revere their wilderness land, warmed by a mellow ocean current and by the inner fires of the earth, and thronged with game. But even more, perhaps, do they revere the forest rivers which link their savage kingdom together, and form their avenues of inter-tribal trade—and oftimes of bloody war.

On the banks of the Hiwasi there is an image of a human head, carved in the rugged granite high on the cliffs through which the river flows.

The head upon the rock is handsome—a skilled, true likeness of a youth, carved by a primitive sculptor. If asked, the sculptor would say, "That is Kioga of Hopeka-town. He did a brave deed."

What he would not say, because he did not know, was that Kioga, known as the Snow Hawk, was Lincoln Rand, the last survivor of a shipwrecked explorer.

ONE AGAINST A WILDERNESS

William L. Chester

DAW BOOKS, INC.

DONALD A. WOLLHEIM, PUBLISHER

1301 Avenue of the Americas
New York, N. Y.   10019

FIRST PRINTING, FEBRUARY 1977

1 2 3 4 5 6 7 8 9

PRINTED IN U.S.A.

TABLE OF CONTENTS

I. The Eyes of Mialoka Will
   Burn Tonight   7

II. The Dire Wolves' Prey   38

III. Unharmed, He Dwelt Among
    the Forest People   72

IV. Flight of the Forest People   97

V. White Heritage   123

VI. The Turn of the Tide   147

Publisher's Note

KIOGA OF THE WILDERNESS left its hero and his friends still lost from us in far Nato'wa. An expedition has sailed to their rescue; but while we await its return, let us enjoy these stories of Kioga's boyhood, told by him to his friend Dr. James Munro during the Snow Hawk's sojourn in America.

PART I

The Eyes of Mialoka
Will Burn Tonight

In far Nato'wa—that new-found land within the Arctic Circle—deep in the still, primeval forest called by the red-skinned natives Indegara, there stands a great rock called Chieftain's Head, supposed to be the image of Mialoka, legendary First-Chief of all the Shoni tribes. When the eyes of Chieftain's Head light up, Two-Star, the little son of Mialoka, will return to take his place among mortal men, so goes the legend, implicitly believed among the Shoni.

Below this rock, towering sentrylike a hundred feet above the neighboring forest, three rushing rivers meet. Their meeting-place is known as the Caldrons of the Yei, a name which well describes the foamy chaos into which the mingling rivers churn each other. Two of these rivers are glacier-born; the third springs from its sources boiling, heated by volcanic fires; and where hot and frigid waters meet, there hangs above the Caldrons a pillar of dense gray mist.

Little is known of this lone, unearthly place, reverberant with the hollow roar of waters through the scoured-out caves which honeycomb its rim. But of one thing the Shoni witch-doctors long were certain: Human bodies, of enemy or village-sacrifice, consigned to the Caldrons, were never seen again. The hungry Yei—mythical spirits of the rivers—ate them, so the Indians believed.

What the Caldrons finally discard at their southern edges is sucked into the vortex of a mighty cataract beyond, then smashed and swept into eternity ... For centuries no human foot had ever pressed this place of peril, nor human eye looked on its inner mysteries and returned to tell of what it saw. . . .

One day, not many years ago, somewhere between Hopeka and the Caldrons of the Yei, a forest denizen stood belly-deep, fishing in the Hiwasi River. More clown than fisherman, the great brown bear leaped among the shining salmon arrowing upstream to their spawning-beds.

Not once in fifty times did his swinging claw-armed paw hook out a shimmering fish. More often the clumsy bruin missed, and fairly stood upon his head amid the silvery horde.

From somewhere near the brush-grown bank a peal of care-free laughter echoed forth. The bruin's small red eyes turned toward the sound, beholding in the shadows a familiar human figure, of a youth of perhaps fifteen. In one strong hand he grasped a pointed chipping-stone, and in the other a half-finished arrow-head, one edge cunningly sharpened, the other still quite dull. Pausing in his primitive task, he laughed again.

Discomfited, perhaps, the bear regained his poise, reared up, and with a sudden lucky pass scooped a big salmon high in air, batting it fiercely toward the bank before it fell.

By sheerest chance the salmon hurtled toward the standing figure. Quick as the flick of sparrow's wing the supple youth dodged, twisting to one side. But for all his haste the writhing fish got in one flat resounding blow, delivered stingingly. The outline of a salmon's tail glowed redly on a brown bare hip.

Much hurt and out of dignity,—of which the middle teens may have great store,—the figure leaped down upon the flopping fish, which got away. Then belated self-command ensued. He turned back to the bank. Standing,—by painful preference,—he meditated on the perils of his wilderness.

The feathers of the Snow Hawk—or Kioga, to call him by his Shoni name—were ruffled. Aki, his wild companion, was laughing at him silently, if expression meant anything at all. High on the bank, with lolling tongue, a fox grinned down on him. Kioga flung a stick—and missed the mark. All things went wrong this day! Again he stood straight and silent as the trees beyond him.

Tall for his fifteen years, already Kioga gave promise of the man he was to be. Lithe and graceful, with long leopard-muscles, he almost matched a full-grown warrior in strength. In quickness and agility, he far excelled the practiced wrestlers and runners of the Shoni tribes—a nation of athletes.

Eager to forget his earlier embarrassment, Kioga plunged forthwith into the river. For a while he wrestled and gamboled with his friendly partner the bear. As if born and existing only to guard him from harm, time and again the huge brute dragged him bodily upon the bank. And soon Kioga forgot his earlier uncomfortable experience in the excitement of diving to elude his burly companion. In the liquid element the lad Kioga was as adept, and elusive, almost, as the salmon. Aki was no match for such tactics.

So for an hour amusement crowded all other thoughts from his mind. Suddenly Kioga felt the bruin stiffen, nostrils twitching toward upstream. Kioga too, chin-deep in water, grew still, clutching Aki's shaggy coat. Presently his own nostrils, little less sharp than his wild companion's, caught the scent of smoke-tanned garments, worn on the backs of men.

"Come, Aki!" whispered Kioga urgently, pressing the rough shoulder. If not in true obedience, then solely to be with him, the bear swam quietly ashore. The Snow Hawk, still hanging on, went with him, without an effort.

Then from below the bank two pairs of watchful eyes observed a tall canoe move into their line of vision. On the forward seat a withered dried-up figure sat—Inkato the shaman, famed and feared for the power of his magic. Hideous with self-mutilation, he sat with scarce a movement, only his glittering eyes denying him to be a mummy.

Behind Inkato a slim boy about ten years old sat pale-faced, with eyes of fear, thongs binding arms behind him immovably.

Astern a lesser shaman propelled the craft downriver, and when the captive struggled, struck him callously with the flat of the paddle.

Watching through slitted lids, behind which the greenish eyes blazed like melting emeralds, the Snow Hawk growled back in his throat. And on a deeper, gruffer note the brute beside him did the same—Kioga's foes were Aki's too.

Well Kioga knew where and to what fate the youthful victim went. For one black mark stands against the Seven Tribes. Whereas their music and arts are things to marvel at, the age-old custom of human sacrifice still survives.

But a wrinkle of perplexity deepened between Kioga's eyes. On some pretext or other, the shamans had decreed death for this unlucky captive. But why such unaccustomed secrecy? Why no chants, no beat of drums, no myriad witnesses to the high ceremony of human sacrifice? Ofttimes before his keen young eyes had seen the hapless victim knifed and hurled headlong into the churning waters—but never in such furtive fashion. Always the village witch-doctors had been on hand in full grotesque regalia.

Clearly something was afoot, something too dark and dread, almost, to think about, if all the other village shamans were not supposed to know of it.

The canoe passed near the recent play-spot. The victim's eyes turned momentarily shoreward, as if seeking a way of escape in that direction. The quickness of his indrawn breath sent the eyes of Inkato also shoreward. With a start he hissed back to his assistant: "Kansa! Saw you some one disappearing in the bush?"

"I glimpsed a bear," said the other.

"No human leg with fish-tail mark upon it?" persisted Inkato.

"Not so. Perhaps I looked too late."

"My lying eyes betrayed me," muttered the old shaman uneasily. "But there is no time to lose. The Yei are hungry. Push on!"

Behind him the luckless little captive slumped lower, stoicism crushed by fear of death.

Push on the second shaman did, until the mighty millrace just above the Caldrons came into view. On either side black basalt walls reared up, cracked and broken. Ahead, the pall of mist above the Caldrons eddied densely, shrouds-to-be of the Shoni boy.

"Now!" came Inkato's voice, instinct with cruelty. With a quick swing, Kansa flung the victim overside, holding the prey afloat while the older shaman crept back with keen knife drawn.

Up went the corded old hand, the bone blade gleaming.

Then suddenly something pale, oval and speckled—the great egg of an emperor goose—hurtled from above. The wielder of the knife shrank back—too late! The half-pound egg, too long unhatched, burst hard against his temple, its evil-smelling contents spattering, and streaming down Inkato's grimacing face.

To the hurler of that egg, the boyish victim's face was not unknown. He was a lad from Hopeka—the name escaped Kioga—recently stricken dumb when lightning struck near where he stood.

Startled, the younger shaman released his grip. Caught in the currents, the bound body was drawn beyond his reach. With eyes of fury Inkato watched it go.

"No matter," he muttered finally. "The Yei take them dead or alive. And they return no sacrifice. Back, careless fool! The current pulls us!"

And Inkato, himself fearful of the death he meted out so casually to others, seized a paddle, forgetful even of the stench which hung about his head. A moment later, mouthing malediction on the mother of that pungent egg, the two were gone upstream, their ends achieved, so far as they could know.

But Inkato was wrong: Whereas the river-Yei had swallowed up the victim, they did not quite digest the mouthful.

Near where the mists were swirling, a second body struck the surface like a flying lance, glancing deeply. Beside the unconscious sacrifice a head appeared. Its owner might have been a river-Yei in person, up from the depths to claim the slender body; for around one strong fist the younger lad's braid was twisted.

A moment, his supple strength against the coiling sinews of three mighty rivers, Kioga fought the currents. Alone he might have had a chance, as does the reed that bends before a hurricane. But encumbered thus, the waters had their way with him.

Tenacity, however, was in his fiber. The will to survive blazed with a fierce white flame—else he had never lived this long. His grip upon that braid tightened in a hold that only death would slacken. And in his dire extremity, one single name escaped him, loud as healthy lungs could shout it out:

"Aki! *Aki!* Aĸɪ!"

A momentary hush ensued, broken only by the sound of rushing waters. Then came a roar like rolling thunder, a splash close by as if a ton of rock had fallen, and a great wave covered Kioga and his burden. When shaggy fur came beneath his hand, the Snow Hawk clutched it, clinging like a limpet.

Now vast primordial strength was laboring for

him—five hundred pounds of solid buoyant brawn, delivering power through four thrusting paws. Gasping stertorously, the bear obliquely stemmed the hungry eddies, slowly neared the carved-out caves.

Dragged coughing to the surface, Kioga caught a breath of air. He had but one thought, to keep his hold on that dark braid and on Aki; only one command to utter fiercely through clenched teeth: "Swim, Aki—*swim!*"

The loyal, selfless heart, already pumping near to bursting, responded, drawing on unknown reserves of power. Seeming hours were but minutes. The thrashing claws scraped bottom, gripped, hooked onto stone, and held. Then surging mightily, Aki dragged himself ashore.

Kioga felt his grip loosening, and again the currents struggled to possess him. Then the patient bruin did him violence, taking one forearm in gin-trap jaws and dragging him for the hundredth time to solid ground—and with Kioga came that other limp, shackled body.

Kioga came to, consciousness rising from a sea of pain. A warm moist roughness licked soothingly across his naked chest. A hot breath thawed his tense and rigid muscles. He saw a vast dark shape bulking huge beside him, and rose up spent and trembling, his first thought for the one he had rescued.

Beside Kioga, at full stretch, the body lay without a movement. The Snow Hawk wore no knife, nor aught else either; but with a chip of stone he sawed through the leather cords, loosened the boy's apparel, and began to chafe the victim back to life.

Swift moments passed; the rescued one showed signs of life. A ray of pale auroral light came through the opening of the cave and fell upon a thin wan face, colored slightly with returning blood—a face of innocence, marked by an ugly bruise on one temple.

More gently now Kioga chafed anew, luring the boy back to consciousness. And as he worked, his eyes narrowed; amazement, resentment, anger grew within him—then black and bitter hatred of those who had worked this crime against a helpless child.

The common bond of youth made that offense seem greater. Until this hour Kioga had loathed the brethren who devised such acts of horror—but with a detached and general kind of loathing. Face to face with dread reality, his hatred crystallized and sought some one on whom to fasten. He thought of the two who had brought the sacrifice downriver—old Inkato and Kansa, his confederate.

"They fed the Yei in secret," he muttered hotly, devising a thousand mental tortures for the guilty pair. "I wonder why? But they'll pay! Blood for thy blood, little brother!"

What the rousing sacrifice thought, waking in that reverberant cave to see a bloody figure crouched above him and a dripping bear near by, can not be known. If fear, Kioga sought to calm it.

"Be not afraid," he shouted in Shoni, above the roar of waters. "None may do you hurt while I am near. I am Kioga—the outcast of Hopeka!"

Then wasting no time on further useless talk, Kioga armed himself with a rock and explored about him, seeking means of egress from this cave-pierced shore of the Caldrons. Aki shuffled after him.

One ledge ended at a whirlpool. Above, sheer rock, slippery with condensing mist, offered no encouragement. The foam-capped waters—he had no wish to challenge them again! Returning, he found another route, along connecting caves, and passed from one to another in an upstream direction. Somewhere, soon, he thought, the area of the Caldrons must abut upon the neighboring forest. But the underground path he followed ended in a wall.

In disappointment he hurled his stone against it. Some slabs of rock, weakened by erosion, slid from the wall. He hurled the stone again; a threat of air, cool and dry, blew through from somewhere, bringing with it scent of pine and hemlock. Encouraged, Kioga hammered afresh, desisting only when his stone fell apart in his hands. With naked hands he tugged and strained. But for all his efforts, he had only made an opening large enough to get one hand through. One huge slab moved slightly. If that could only be moved a little more—

Behind him Aki sneezed with the sound as of a parting compressed-air coupling. Kioga jumped in surprise—but with a great idea dawning. Directing the bear's attention to the opening, "Smell, Aki!" he commanded. The brute sniffed eagerly, caught the scent of outer liberty and understood. Exerting all his strength, he pulled upon that slab. Kioga also pulled. With a rumble the slab fell inward. The way was clear.

A few minutes later Kioga carried the Shoni boy out, carefully concealing the new-made en-

trance to the Caldrons; for here was another retreat in time of peril.

Guarded on his way by one no other wilderness
brute dared face, Kioga moved north and west-
ward through the forest labyrinths, never hesitat-
ing, though changing direction a hundred times.

From thicket, cave and deep ravine, eyes saw
the little trio pass—eyes that were bright as heated
coins, eyes like mirrors reflecting flame, many only
curious, many more hot with hungry menace. The
Shoni boy shivered in fear.

Kioga soothed him, bantering a little. "Fear not,
little brother. Who dares molest Kioga and his
friends? What is thy name?" he asked; then as he
spoke he remembered that the boy was dumb.
But to his surprise, the other answered:

"I am Ohali. My father is a chief. My brothers
all are warriors."

"But you were dumb! I heard the shamans say
it."

"When the river took me, I cried out. My voice
came back."

"Why did the shamans give thee to the Yei?"

Ohali shivered. "I do not know. They seized me
in the night. I struggled, but could not cry out."

A gust of fury swept Kioga afresh, tearing out
this vow: "They'll pay! Before the sun and moon
and all the stars, I swear it!"

"Where are we going? Back—where Inkato and
Kansa are?"

Kioga heard the boy's teeth chatter. "Not so,
little brother. While Inkato and Kansa live, you'll
not be safe in all Hopeka. Yet since they did not
kill thee, why should I kill them? There must be
a better way. First we will rest and eat."

"Where do you live?" Ohali asked.

"Where once a tiger couched. That is Kioga's home."

In awe Ohali heard these words. "Who are you?"

Thoughtfully Kioga answered, putting into words dim thoughts, maturing ideals of youth at shining manhood's threshold: "I am a friend to all like thee, Ohali. I place small birds back in the nest. I kill no doe with young. I aid the weak, destroy the wicked strong and make them fear me. Hast ever heard of Robin Hood?"

"Ra-bin-hud?" echoed Ohali, repeating the English words with unaccustomed lips. Smiling, Kioga bade him forget the question.

"A friend of mine you would not know, Ohali."

Perplexed, the thin young arms, dark with the marks of cutting thongs, tightened round Kioga's neck. "I do not fear Kioga."

"Nor I the shamans," muttered Kioga. But Ohali heard him not. He was asleep.

Presently Kioga turned off the trail, climbed a steep narrow path to a point halfway up a frowning cliff. Pausing before a mat of growing vines, he pushed them aside, exposing a huge log door chinked with mud and mosses. Manipulating a latch, Kioga pushed in the door and entered, placing his burden gently on a pile of thick soft furs.

With curving stick and leather thong he kindled sparks and blew them into flame and made a fire. A veritable pirate's den, that cave, hung all about with bows and arrows, coils of leather rope, long whips that were the dread of every brute that prowled the forest, and many kinds of Indian garments, and hideous devil-masks.

One of the garments Kioga fastened round his waist with cord of buckskin. The slight demands of modesty thus satisfied, he went forth through the night again, returning in an hour, laden with nuts and berries and wild birds' eggs.

Upon the coals he set an earthen pot, filled with water from a rock-spring bubbling in the recesses of his cave: and into this flung quantities of dried meat and vegetables from his basket stores.

Then, beholding Ohali's tattered garments, from a leather case he pulled out fringed buckskin shirt and leggings of hide, cured soft and white, with moccasins to match—his own gala boy's attire, long since outgrown but treasured none the less, because a loved one's fingers had sewn upon them. These, with other ornaments he placed where Ohali must see them when he first awoke.

His body stretched to rest before the bubbling stew, Kioga pondered: How return Ohali to Hopeka without delivering him back into the hands of Inkato—who, one way failing, would find other means of persecuting the boy?

Still wrestling with that problem, Kioga slept—in utter weariness.

Meanwhile, pulling for Hopeka town upon the Hiwasi River, Inkato had rested uneasily upon his paddle.

"A leg with fish-tail mark upon it—I cannot put that out of mind," he told his companion. "Let us go back and look along the shore. If it were known we did this thing—"

Then came Kansa's voice, guttural and deep: "What have we gained by this great risk? Because his father cursed you when his son was stricken dumb—was that cause enough to take Ohali's life?"

"We did not *take* a life," corrected Inkato, drawing a fine distinction. "We *gave* it—unto the Yei. You see things crookedly, O Kansa. I fear you will never be a famous shaman."

"What would our fellow-shamans say, learning that we did this secretly, without their knowledge?"

"How will they ever know—unless you babble, Kansa? Cease sniveling!"

Uneasily Kansa shook his head, pushing downstream toward the point where movement had earlier caught the older shaman's eye. When they had arrived, Inkato spoke.

"Go you ashore and look about. I will watch, with bow in hand, to see that no harm befalls you."

Kansa took up his spear and disembarked, scanning the bank on every hand. Then suddenly he straightened with a hiss. "The footprints of a bear, I see—and others, manlike but smaller than a warrior's."

"I knew it!" cried the old villain fiercely. "We were seen—and know you who made those tracks?"

Kansa shook his head, wondering at the other's agitation.

"Kioga!" snarled Inkato, the weapons quivering in his hand. "He who runs with the bears of Indegara!"

"*Agh!*" choked Kansa, his face losing color. "What if he saw us throw Ohali into the river!"

"That egg—I should have known!" remembered Inkato. "Back to the Caldrons, Kansa! Make haste! Methinks there is no good in this!"

The startled shamans returned to the scene of their outrage. And after searching long, they came upon fresher tracks, again of youth and bear together. One look at the human spoor, and Inkato stiffened. "He carried a burden. And look you, Kansa—all are wet. There's mud within the prints. And here—two smaller prints!"

"Ohali lives," muttered Kansa. "We are betrayed!"

Inkato shook his head defiantly. "Not yet, you shivering fool. Back to Hopeka—bend your paddle, Kansa, or it may be you will never bend it again!"

Awaking in the cave, the first object Kioga's eyes fell upon was Ohali, standing straight and slender, clad all in new white buckskin, capped with crown of hawk-wing plumes, on either wrist a ruddy copper bracelet; and glittering and flashing in the firelight, fine beadwork upon his breast and back.

A spark of inspiration touched Kioga off.

"*Ahai!* I see the way!"

"What way?" demanded Ohali, puzzled by the words.

"The way to put Ohali beyond the reach of such as Inkato. Hast heard the legend, that when the eyes of Mialoka, the First Chief, are seen to burn, the son of Mialoka will return to dwell with living men?"

"*Ahi,*" answered Ohali, not understanding.

"You shall be Mialoka's son. The eyes of Mialoka will burn tomorrow night!"

Ohali had shivered at mention of the shaman Inkato. His poise was swiftly gone, and fear looked from his eyes.

Kioga's mind worked swiftly. Were it known what now he contemplated, all Shoni shaman-hood would work against him. Those less fanatic medicine-men who worked with roots and herbs and sought no power in primitive politics, would frown on his scheme. Even the common populace would restrain him.

But there was the measure of Kioga's peculiar daring. Half of his short young life had been an epic struggle—one against a wilderness. A lone hand held no terrors. His wits versus theirs—one brain against a hundred—would be no new experience.

He reprimanded Ohali swiftly. "Shrink not, little brother. Stand proud and straight. From this day forth, the greatest chiefs will do thee honor. Far and near thy fame will spread." And with the words, Kioga laughed aloud and said again: "The eyes of Mialoka will burn tomorrow night. And henceforward men will know Ohali as Two Star, son of the First Chief!"

Bewildered by this rapid flow of words, Ohali straightened once again. "How can this be?"

Pursing his lips and drawing in his cheeks grotesquely, Kioga spoke as Inkato was wont to boast: "I am Kioga, greatest of all magicians!" Then again he laughed outright, and Ohali laughed with him, scarcely knowing why, save that with Kioga near he could not long be fearful or unhappy.

When their meal was done, Kioga showed Ohali tricks of sleight-of-hand; and while Ohali sat entranced, squatted there before the little lad, telling funny tales to make him laugh, and drawing pictures on a buffalo-hide for Ohali's amusement—and for his own delight as well; for when

Ohali's laughter bubbled up, Kioga listened raptly, as a long-deaf person might who heard a sudden note of flutelike music. Not often had Kioga human friend to share his solitude . . .

Sometimes, though, a shadow crossed Ohali's face—a face too young to bear such marks of haunting fear. Then pity filled the Snow Hawk's heart; and to erase the shadow, he called in Aki from his guard-post outside the door, and to the trill of Pan-pipes made Aki rear and dance, and bear Ohali on his shaggy shoulders.

All in all, it was a merry evening, ending far too soon in weariness. Ohali slept as never in his life before.

Banking the fire, Kioga again quit the cave, then to the broad Hiwasi went, sought out his hidden bark canoe and on the central stronger current came swiftly toward Hopeka town. Hiding his canoe, Kioga neared the palisaded village afoot, gained secret ingress, and prowling the shadows of the long-houses came to the lodge of Inkato the shaman.

Listening, he heard no sound within. Entering stealthily—no lodge is ever barred among the Shoni—Kioga found a fire glowing, by whose light his darting gaze saw many things. Above the coals a cooking-vessel simmered, of which Kioga smelled, turning up his nose. To one side hung a bunch of shriveled berries—a violent medicine, whose attributes Kioga well remembered.

On a wicked impulse he flung these into the cooking-pot, adding also to the broth some other near-by ingredients, which the shamans never prescribed for themselves. Then stirring slowly, he sniffed again, adding more of this and that until the odor satisfied him by its vileness.

Hearing footsteps, he hastily retreated through a side entrance to the lodge and hid himself outside, ear glued to the barken wall. Soon some one entered. He heard the lisp of Inkato's voice, speaking to a companion through toothless jaws.

"*Ehi-ehi!* A lucky thing we found their footprints. Tomorrow we will track them down with warriors from the village. All will think Kioga stole Ohali from the village. And when we come upon them, we will kill the Snow Hawk. And if," added the shaman meaningly, "Ohali is also killed, it will be by accident—will it not, Kansa—eh?"

"It will need doing quickly," answered Kansa darkly, "lest Ohali himself betray us."

"Then see you carry springy bow and sharp arrows. Leave Kioga to my spear."

Outside the lodge Kioga listened, missing not a word. Beyond doubt the shamans knew Ohali was still alive. If they had their way, he would bear the blame for the boy's kidnaping, and all his plans would go awry. To return and efface the trail to the cave could yet be done, but that required time. What other way? What better, quicker way?

Much that had been not clear before was now explained. The outrage they had perpetrated on the river had not even the slight redeeming color of religious sacrifice. It had been attempted child-murder, brutal, vicious, and hidden even from the other medicine-men.

Among the Shoni there is no penalty for the taking of a life. By custom, as among the old-time

Iroquois, the killer waits beside the body of his victim, until discovered. Life may call for life; or a gift to the nearest of the dead man's kin to satisfy the spirit of the departed. Thus the elements of primitive honor prevail.

Not so with Inkato and Kansa. Their crime was so far without the pale that not even their own fraternity must know, much less the family of Ohali. Upon this fact the quick wits of the Snow Hawk seized at once. His problem was resolving rapidly.

But once more Inkato was speaking, as if he had not recently returned from doing foulest deed: "Come, Kansa! Fill the bowls. My belly is an empty gourd."

Through a crack Kioga saw Kansa approach the cooking-pot, fill one bowl, then sniff the contents doubtfully.

"This soup—how strange it smells! I think—" began Kansa, but Inkato cut him short indignantly.

"Rich and full of strength! Fresh this very morning. Drink heartily, O Kansa, and mayhap it will make you great—like Inkato!" And snatching the brimming bowl the old shaman emptied it in greedy gulps.

Not daring to offend his host afresh, Kansa held his nose and also drank. The two put down their bowls and sat in silence.

Then Inkato to Kansa spoke: "Why is your face so pale?"

Kansa made a sickly grimace, answering in a stranger's voice, "I would have asked the same—of you."

Inkato gave a sudden mighty start, clutching at his middle.

And presently, grinning with satisfaction, Kioga

went away. One hour, at least, would pass before these two could go about again. . . .

This time Kioga visited the longest tongue in all Hopeka town. He found her crouched before her lodge and stood above her quietly.

"Some one is near," said the old crone harshly. "Who is it?"

"Who brought thee sweets and cakes and wood to burn and water from the spring, when others all forsook thee, Mother Iska?"

A moment she was silent, her blind mask softening. Then: "Kioga, lightener of my sightless misery! How dare you enter Hopeka, where so many wish you ill? What would you have of eyeless Iska? But ask, and it is yours."

He pressed her gnarled old claws tenderly. "I ask no gift. I bring you one. The gift you love the best," Kioga answered.

"Something to whisper in my ear!" she exclaimed in excitement, bending nearer avidly. For news, the spoken word, twenty kinds of gossip—all these made Iska's darkened world endurable.

"A juicy something," Kioga agreed, and sitting close beside old Iska, spoke long and earnestly—just as in years gone by he had brought her other choice gems of information.

In rapt attention she heard him. "Eh-eh-eh? Go on—go on!" And as he spoke, she stiffened. "O hearts more black than midnight! What do you say to me, Kioga?"

" 'Tis true," he assured her. "With these two eyes I saw them throw Ohali in. In these ears he told me all that I tell thee. *The eyes of Mialoka will burn tomorrow night!*"

"O wonder!" Old Iska fairly trembled with the

weight of this disclosure. "It will shake all Hopeka. And I,"—her face lit up with joy,—"sightless, aged, crippled old Iska, I alone know it is to happen. . . . Ask any boon for this great gift, Kioga!"

"Some other time, Mother," he said. "But tell this to no living soul," Kioga admonished mysteriously, the more certainly to insure a wide broadcast of all he had confided.

Then leaving excited Iska, Kioga returned without misadventure to his canoe and hurried downstream toward the Caldrons, approaching Chieftain's Head on foot from its one accessible side.

Along the broad ledge that simulates a human brow, and in the hollows so like eyes, he heaped a pile of brush and firewood, ready to be kindled with a spark. That done, he returned again to his forest cave, found all there well, and had four hours of sleep before the morning dawned.

Rising with the sun, Kioga woke Ohali, broke fast on fruit and some acorn-cakes smuggled from Hopeka, and told him of his activities. "Iska knows that you are alive. Iska will tell the whole village. The people will await the coming of Two-Star back to this earth. And then it will be the turn of Kansa and Inkato to shiver in their blankets!"

But poor Ohali did not seem to feel enthusiastic, and to lighten his fears Kioga took down a book from a covered shelf. This and many other volumes he had salvaged from the cabin of a sinking hulk off the seashore; and from it he read to Ohali a tale of Sherwood Forest, translating the English as best he could for Ohali. Thus also had

Mokuyi done when teaching Kioga to read and speak English, the mother tongue. And hearing the strange stories of an unknown civilized world, Ohali calmed again.

Then Kioga put the book aside, and after a moment of silence asked: "Hast ever seen a river-Yei, Ohali?"

"No," answered the Shoni boy. "But they look like men, with devils' heads. So my father told me."

"And hands webbed like a duck's, and great brown spots upon their bodies," added Kioga reflectively.

"Have *you* seen one?" asked Ohali curiously.

"No," said Kioga, "though I have poked long poles in every river-hole seeking to bring one forth."

Ohali's eyes grew great. "You dared—do that?"

"Aki was with me," explained Kioga. "Together we fear nothing. And tomorrow," continued Kioga, "the Shoni will see a river-Yei. Now listen well, Ohali."

Rounder still grew Ohali's great dark eyes, as the Snow Hawk spoke. And when Kioga had done: "I dare not—I dare not!" whispered Ohali, pale with fear again.

"If I am close behind, Ohali—then will you dare?"

Ohali's fears grew less. Return to home and family in prospect, and with the Snow Hawk his ally? "Yes—yes!" he said at last.

"Good, little warrior," commented Kioga. "Now watch."

On a buckskin he drew the outlines of his hands, and with a whetted knife cut out four pieces; and sewed the four together with needle of bone and sinew thread, into the shape of overlarge gloves, save that he left the fingers joined together like the toes of Paddle-foot, the wild duck.

Next from the wall he took down his most hideous medicine-mask, fringed about the open neck with human hair and made to be worn upon the head like a helmet. Then taking deer-grease in a small stone cup, he added to it reddish earthy pigment, mixing the two together.

These several adjuncts to his ambitious schemes he wrapped up in a deer-skin, fastening the bundle to the shoulders of faithful Aki. Then he set leisurely forth, whip in belt, and Ohali by his side, toward his canoe.

Along the way Aki, guardian of their every previous step, roamed off the trail, lured by some vagrant scent or other. Where the forest paths were open, Ohali walked beside Kioga. In tangled places the Snow Hawk lifted him easily in his arms, moving by leaps and bounds if he were no weight at all. Now and then he dropped from cliff to bough, while Ohali hung tightly on, certain that they must plummet far to earth.

But nothing like that happened. Impossible places passed easily beneath his knowing feet; and once indeed, they took six long drops in quick succession. But by now Ohali knew no further fear and enjoyed the swift exhilarating descent.

Almost to the river grave hazard growled fiercely at them from a trail-side cave. With back-laid ears and lashing tail, a great snow-leopard appeared.

Were Aki here, he had not dared venture forth. Now, unmenaced, in another instant he would spring, and rend.

Ohali, standing mesmerized by the golden cat's fire-circled stare, was struck rigid with terror. Not so Kioga.

Before the brute was halfway out, he flicked his length of leather whip behind him. Then, with a move too quick for eye to follow, the long lash slithered forward. Beneath the leopard's hanging jaw the hissing whang-strip barked like an exploded pistol. Then twice again—*crack! crack!*—the long lash made the fur fly up.

Checked in full intent to spring, the stung leopard arched up its spine and hissing like any common alley cat, broke ground before the baffling thong. One more resounding *whack* and the brute turned. And when the lash flicked forth again, the beast was gone.

Gone, too, in another moment, were Kioga and Ohali, who reached the canoe without further incident. Aki found them there, delivered up his shoulder pack, and when the little craft turned downriver, swam powerfully, close behind.

When they had gone a little way, Kioga let the craft drift of its own volition, and reaching into the bundle, took forth the deer-fat paint he had mixed in the cave, handing it to Ohali.

"Now paint me," he said, "so that if any Yei should see me, he would come and call me brother."

In Hopeka events transpired as Kioga had hoped. As always, the Hopeka women paused, to visit a while with the poor blind Iska, human clearing-house of village information.

Unable to contain her wondrous secret, the aged crone let slip—a word here, a word there—the burning rumor Kioga had confided to her.

The village women, filled with wonder, told other women, in strictest confidence. *"The eyes of Mialoka will burn tonight!"* To those who doubted, "Iska told me," they said, by way of proof. The gossip-pot boiled up; the lid blew off. Like swift wildfire, then, the news flew round. Ohali was in truth, said Iska, the son of First-Chief, come humbly back to earth in the guise of a minor chieftain's child. Ohali's mother, hearing, grew faint.

Corn-cakes burned; meals grew cold; clothing went unmended.

And in his lodge cruel Inkato and Kansa his confederate, ill as men could ever be, lay groaning on the floor. An hour passed before they recovered from the effects of Kioga's potpourri.

Kansa, going to the door, returned with tidings that made Inkato's own blood flow swiftly once again. "The village folk are rising! There is a wondrous stir. Strange rumors are afloat: Iska spreads them even now. 'Tis said Ohali is not mortal child but the son of the First-Chief, Mialoka!"

Up to his feet sprang Inkato. Quivering to vague apprehensions, they looked at one another. "Quick! Knives and tomahawks. Mayhap even now we have waited too long."

Inkato quivered, recalling Ohali's warrior-brothers, his chieftain father, and all those eager knives that waited.

But he was quick to recover a measure of his composure. "Come!" he said to Kansa. "Let us look and listen, and learn what is going on."

To accomplish that, the shamans had but to follow the crowd in their own canoe, downriver.

Along the broad Hiwasi, the village canoes had

gathered thickly, filled with Indians from Hopeka. No torch yet blazed above the curving prows. All was dusk within shadow. There came the click and buzz of whispered conversation. Hundreds of dark eyes fastened upon a distant lofty point—the crown of Chieftain's Head, above the Caldrons, coming slowly into view.

"The legend is come true! The eyes of Mialoka burn!"

Suddenly a cry of awe—the eyes far overhead were lighting uncannily: a halo glowed about the rocky mist-draped crown; smoke poured from the stony lips. It was the sign, the portent of some great happening, which blind old Iska had foretold!

Bemused, enthralled by wonder, the Shoni saw the burning eyes grow dim, the fiery chaplet fade against the sky.

The prow- and helmsmen breathed upon their punk-wood tinder, preparing. As the last glow dimmed on Chieftain's Head, they fanned their sparks to flame and lit the smoking torchlights stem and stern. For thus had blind old Iska earlier counseled them to do.

Quivering shadows wriggled on the coaly waters. The river, dark before, became a sea of yellowish light, save where a rocky point threw ebon shade from shore to shore.

Then something pale and ghostly seemed to float from nowhere. The outlines of a small canoe were seen. Within, a dimly gleaming figure knelt. As the craft came slowly forward, this was seen to be a youth in full regalia. Forth from the gloomy shades his craft of beauty came—canoe of birch-bark white as snow. Forward knelt the figure, robed in frosty cloud. And as the torchlights illumined him, his gala raiment seemed on fire.

Wide-eyed and open-mouthed, the watchers stared, bedazzled.

Then some one sharp of eye saw and recognized: "Ohali—Ohali! 'Tis he, indeed! Ohali is the son of Mialoka!"

From behind Ohali, hitherto almost unseen, a crouching thing of horror reared its goblin head—not head of man but more like devil. Its hands seemed not as common hands, but webbed as if for swimming. Its human body, lithe and muscular, was mottled with great liver-colored spots. No thing like this had ever walked the earth before—yet children among the assemblage well knew it for the ogre with whose name women frighten small offenders.

"A Yei—a river-Yei," they whispered. "Go not too near!"

While they watched, the Yei with webbed hands propelled the snow-white craft along, pausing now and then to jabber weirdly. Thus, with its cargo of comely youth and unearthly terror, the white canoe moved among the village craft. Its white-clad youth half-smiled. Its hideous ogre made furious clutching passes ever and anon, whereat the nearest women screamed and shrank away.

But seeing that no harm befell, a few canoes drew nearer, among them one containing Inkato and Kansa.

As the shamans neared, the foremost figure in the white canoe whispered, "I am afraid."

From behind him came an answer, "Fear not! Behold, they look at us in awe."

In the foremost canoe a stately figure spoke, with trembling hand outstretched. "Ohali, my son, we know not if you live or are a spirit."

Astern the goblin river-Yei muttered something. The youth then spoke in low tones—yet not one was there but heard the words distinctly: "Are you not my father Tenasi?"

A cry of awe rose up. "Miracle! Miracle! Ohali the dumb has answered! Ohali's tongue is loosened!"

Answering uncertainly, Tenasi said: "Once I called Ohali my son. But now he returns from the Caldrons, whence never human body returned before. He comes as the legend says the son of Mialoka will return. He comes back to life as Two-Star. None knew of this until blind old Iska foretold it."

Astern the river-Yei shook and choked, as in convulsion.

"The Yei cannot breathe well when out of water," a Shoni mother whispered to her son near by. "Like fish they are, with gills."

Then rose a warrior seated behind Tenasi, and said, as spokesman for his brothers: "We are your earthly brothers. What happened to Ohali?"

"He was given to the Yei," came the answer, and gesturing toward the stern: "One of their number brings me back to you."

A great indrawn breath sounded among the people. The canoe containing Inkato and Kansa moved slightly nearer. Both shamans' eyes were glued in fascination upon the white-clothed figure, whose face grew deathly pale beneath that scrutiny.

Ominous as distant thunder, the voice of the

chief spoke again: "Who gave Ohali to the river-Yei?"

Still closer moved the shamans' craft. Rigid as an image sat the river-Yei, watching their every move. Muttering something, he heard Ohali repeat—swaying where he sat—

"Two men of wicked hearts."

"Name them," came the fierce appeal from Tenasi. The silent multitude strained their ears to hear. No sound was audible save the distant cough of prowling tiger.

The shaman's craft was only spear-length distant from the white canoe. The eyes of those within it bored into Ohali. Some there were who later said they heard a voice then mutter, "Courage!" Right or wrong, Ohali seemed to stiffen, though his voice fell to a whisper. He answered slowly, "The name of one was—"

Suddenly one in the craft so close beside him sprang up, with frightful yell, and in his back-drawn hand a war-ax gleamed. Ohali did not stir, but gripped the gunwales as if by some command.

In a voice like ice some one unknown finished Ohali's sentence, pronouncing the name he feared to utter: "Kansa!"

Kioga had sought only the disgrace of Kansa, not the penalty of death. But now there was no choice. He acted to save Ohali's life.

Before the younger shaman could strike, Kansa seemed to choke and wither where he stood. Those close by could hear a high-pitched *twang* and see an arrow sticking through his neck. Then Kansa toppled limply into the river. And as he sank the river-Yei watched fixedly.

Again the voice of Tenasi: "Who was the other?"

Again Ohali whispered, "The other's name—was Inkato!"

"*Yala-i!*" Shrill and terrible rose that cry from behind the chief, out of the mouths of Ohali's brothers. "Quick, after him!"

But Inkato had acted swiftly, already swung his craft out into the current, and crouching somewhat forward, presented little target to the spears that glanced the water all around.

Though they might have caught up with him, it was seen to be unnecessary—and dangerous. The shaman raised a startled yell. Slowly but inexorably, the currents were bearing him toward the fate to which he had sent so many others—straight to the Caldrons of the Yei.

In the white canoe Ohali swayed. Up rose the river-Yei to bolster him. Ohali heard swift muffled words close at his ear: "Well done, little brother! They'll trouble thee no more. Good-by, O son of Mialoka."

"Good-by," answered Ohali brokenly, and to the horror of the onlookers, threw impulsive arms about the Yei. "Ohali never will forget."

"Hang on," came Kioga's final word. Ohali gripped the gunwales tightly.

One spring, a knifelike entry with little splash—that quickly the Yei was gone beneath the surface, the same surface which carried Inkato away.

With beating heart Ohali watched for sign of him upon the water. A minute passed—another. Clutching the gunwales, the boy went paler than before. Then from somewhere in the shadows near the bank, there came a loud and imperious call:

"*Ahai!* Aki! Aki!"—followed by a whistle.

Downstream, like rat in sinking trap, Inkato heard that call, and glancing shoreward saw a naked figure vanish from the moon's new light. Seeing, Inkato stared, drop-jawed. On one bare hip he dimly saw the mark of salmon's tail. Then glancing upward he caught a last view of Chieftain's Head and stared anew. For where the fire had burned, the stony face had cracked; the Chieftain seemed to smile. Then mists enwrapped bewildered Inkato, and he was seen no more.

Ohali also heard that imperative summons and a bear's answering call. Hearing, he smiled with happy recollection of a strange exciting adventure.

But Kioga, the Snow-Hawk, climbing the rims and ledges above the Caldrons, his face to the forest and the future, did not look back.

PART II

The Dire Wolves' Prey

Upon a cliff which overlooks a winding forest river, two bare brown figures amused themselves by shooting arrows out across the water. One was a boy of ten or thereabouts, slim, black-eyed, coarse-haired, copper-skinned; the other was somewhat older, by far more lithely muscular, with blue-green eyes and the clear brown skin of a well-tanned Caucasian.

Near by, a great good-natured bear reared up manlike, with small red puzzled eyes, to watch the arrows fly. Beside the older youth a full-grown puma, silver-gray with eyes of blazing ice, rubbed its glossy side against his thighs, and curled its tail about his ankles. When the panther showed its shining fangs the younger boy drew back. His friend admonished him:

Shrink not, Ohali, or Mika will wish to bite. That is the way of all like him. Now Aki, here, is harmless, and lets us ride upon his back—yet he could kill a tiger."

Ohali's eyes widened as his companion spoke,

and he answered in higher tones: "Kioga knows the forest people better than all others."

"Who not, *ehi?*" asked Kioga. "I dwell among them. I know their tongue. I've had a hundred different pets."

"A tiger, even?" asked Ohali.

"Not so," Kioga said with evident regret. "But look you here, Ohali!" And he held forth a piece of leather rope, fashioned into a noose. "With this I soon shall capture one and tame him."

"Capture Guna?" gasped Ohali.

"Or else Gunahi, his mate," assured Kioga grandly. "One or the other, I do not care. Come on! Let's go upstream a way. I'll show thee how I'm sure a tiger may be taken."

"I am afraid," Ohali said, holding back.

"Afraid?" echoed Kioga, looking here and there in scorn. "With Aki at our side? I tell thee, little brother, that is folly. Come, Aki, we will show him."

And with the monster bear rolling on majestically ahead, the pair set blithely forth. As they walked along an animal trail, Kioga whittled a notch into a stick. At last he called a halt near where a good stout sapling grew just off the trail. With monkey skill he climbed it rapidly, and at its apex forced it downward in an arc. But his weight was not enough to bend it down to earth. And so Ohali climbed, more slowly. What with the added weight the tree's crown touched the trail.

Now to that bent-down crown Kioga tied his noose, and to the running end affixed the trigger-stick, and set the trigger-stick into a notch he had cut in a stump beneath it. Most warily he spread the noose raising its sides upon four twigs an inch above the ground. The runway snare was set.

"In a day or two Guna will come along and put his foot into the trap. Then we shall have our tiger," said Kioga. "But now—what's that? I hear the boatmen singing! The trade-canoes are coming! Come, Ohali, we will join them. Begone, Aki! And thou, Mika my lithe one, or the warriors will put arrows between thy ribs."

Responding to some sign unknown to Ohali, the great bear shuffled off. The puma trotted away in another direction.

Upon the river-bank Kioga hailed an oncoming craft.

"Luck to you, warriors! Take us on. We're going to Hopeka."

The pole-men recognized the familiar figure. One canoe passed close to shore, and into it Kioga lifted Ohali. "See thee anon, little brother," he said. "Wokili is coming. I'll ride upon his great craft."

A trade-canoe drew near, with many a friendly quip and smile from the warriors; and leaping from a rock, Kioga came aboard.

The time was dusk of a day in the Moon Before the First Snow Flies. The place was Nato'wa, a newfound Arctic land, unknown to civilized men when these events transpired.... The canoes moved toward old Hopeka-town, chief village of the red-skinned Shoni tribesmen who dwell in the somber forest on the eastern coast of Nato'wa. And as they drew near, a voice rang loud from within the palisade.

The voice was Saki's—unmistakably. From wall

to twelve-foot palisaded wall her lusty cry rang musically:

"*Ohai, ya!* Come look! Come see my wares! *Ohai!*"

The words came from the lips of one whose hair was flecked with many winters' snows. Beneath her garb of shell-beaded buckskin, her body was but a wisp of life, a bag of skin containing bones. All Saki's strength, the villagers declared, had gone into her vocal cords. And once again, incongruously, as if a kitten were to utter a tiger's roar, her strong voice rose from her wizened chest:

"*Ohai! Ya!* Come trade with Saki. *Ohai!*"

The dense pine leafage overhanging the village wall quivered at those penetrating tones. Beyond the tall log walls, and even out upon the gleaming bosom of the ebon river, dark-skinned men drifting downstream in deep-laden trade-canoes heard her, and smiled.

Lighted on their way to Hopeka-town by flares at stem and stern, the trading-craft came on in small flotillas, manned by sweating pole-men, whose naked bodies glistened in the smoky light. Indians these were, surviving cousins of the hunter tribes who roamed America in the ancient days. In cast of face, in color of their skins, no difference could be seen. But in their ways and tribal customs peculiar changes have occurred, nowhere more notably than in the laws of barter and of trade. Because of their form of union—seven tribes under one emperor-chief, linked together by the forest rivers—seasonal bazaars have long been customary, whereat the differing produce of these several tribes is traded and exchanged.

To such a bazaar now went the trading craft.

Some creaked with loads of edibles, grown and harvested in mountain valleys far to the north and brought to Hopeka in baskets large enough to contain a warrior. Others rode deep with glazed pottery and polished cups and brilliant vases that caught the eye. Still more were piled with fragrant woods, savage weaponry and skins of wild animals, all heaped so high that it seemed none could survive the trip downriver without capsizing.

In one of these stout craft, atop a bale of precious skins precariously poised amidships, Kioga came upon all fours, stood gracefully erect in perfect balance upon that shaky footing, his splendid, supple all-but-naked body gilded by the torchlight. Then from his own lips skirled a wild, ear-splitting whistle—his answer to the cry of withered Saki.

And Saki, surrounded by her bursting baskets, and skins displayed, and clothing and maple-sugar, heard him. She showed her toothless gums and cackled at the naked red-skinned children lurking all about her.

"*Eh-hee!* Look out, thieving young crows. Kioga comes to watch when Saki sleeps. He has an arm that's long."

Hardly had she spoken, when Hopeka's gates swung out. Through them, chanting the weird refrain of a riverman's song, came a troop of burdened men, bowed down by the weight of goods for trade at the autumn bazaars.

In their van a supple youth cavorted, an animated coil of flesh and blood turning handsprings like a spinning Catherine-wheel until those who watched grew dizzy. As suddenly the Snow Hawk ceased his nimble antics, and cried out:

"Water for the warriors! *Ahai*, Saki! I am here again!"

Kioga sprang to her side, and with a flourish dropped something in her buckskin lap; a little bunch of forest flowers, to pluck which he had dared a viper's fangs. And as he came near, the ring of village children fell quickly back, for all stood in awe of this strange child of the wilderness.

"Aha, my jumping-bug!" said Saki. "What's this?"

"A nosegay to please thy nostrils, Grandmother," quoth Kioga. "*Ahi*—but I am hungry! What's to eat?"

"O belly that is never full—here's a roasted joint to fill thee up," grumbled Saki, tossing him a haunch of venison.

With ravenous appetite Kioga fell to; and in amazement the old crone watched the deer-meat disappear, and with it two great bowls of steaming soup.

"O jug without a bottom," she marveled as Kioga drew one wrist across his lips, "what news along the river-ways?"

"Great tidings, Grandmother. The traders come by hundreds. The greatest chiefs from all the northern tribes are on the way. In one more week your bazaar will be crowded. But I have also heard some speak of evil men within our tribes."

"Too true! Too true!" declared Saki, casting a furtive glance about her. "The very trees do listen. Something ill is brewing, my son. Sawamic's warriors have been alert—more so than usual, these latter days."

"What do they fear?" asked the youth Kioga.

Again that furtive look, before old Saki answered: "The Long Knives' secret brotherhood, whose members no one knows for certain. Takaso, the double-tongued, is thought to be a leader among them. But trouble not thy good young head with thoughts of this. What else has happened thee, my son?"

"Well," replied Kioga, rocking on the end of his spine and continuing with his river news, "I saw a tiger, fat with young, for one thing. And when a water-snake bit Saya-hala, with my tomahawk I chopped his finger off—*squit!*—like that!"

"*Eh-eh*—did he flinch?" queried Saki.

As they spoke, the village children edged in "A little—the blade was dull. But he gave me twenty arrows just the same, for saving his life. This morning," continued Kioga, "T'yone snarled at me from a bank. With a paddle I knocked one of his teeth out. See!" And with that he displayed the wolf's long fang.

"*Tzik-tzik!* You're never at a loss," declared Saki fondly.

As they spoke, the village children edged in closer, eyeing the articles on display in Saki's bazaar. Kioga went on talking.

"Wokili got an arrow in the back. Ketchawin sneaked into the forest and came back with a scalp. It was a Wa-Kanek's, by the top-knot. But nothing exciting happened.... Oh, Ketchawin brought me a piece of rawhide. With it I fixed my whip. See!" And with a deft movement he flung out ten feet of tapered bull-hide lash, fixed to a springy stock of wood and bone.

Old Saki cried out suddenly, pointing the while

to a village boy who, taking advantage of her pre-occupation, had reached into an open basket. "Ya-ya! He steals!"

Before her words were fairly out, Kioga's bull-hide thong snaked forth. With a cry the little pil-lager drew back. But quicker than any human hand, the lash had caught him, lapping twice about his wrist. Now with one jerk Kioga brought the boy sprawling to the feet of Saki, who belabored him with a stick until he dropped what he had taken, and ran howling away.

Kioga laughed loud and long. "Now, Grand-mother, do thou go and sleep awhile. I will guard thy baskets." And turning a sharp and watchful eye upon the semicircle of village children, Kioga crossed his legs and squatted upon a tall wicker basket, his ready whip in hand. Presently he jeered them.

"Come nearer, crows!" invited Kioga with gleaming eyes. "Come just a little nearer. . . . You will not? Then here!"—tossing a trinket on the earth before them. "Pick it up, crows—pick it up!"

As Kioga spoke, he played the supple lash upon the ground in sinuous undulations, and cracked it with a soft sound, the whisper of its anger-voice. But though covetous lights showed in their eyes, no one among the village children dared reach forth when that quick-striking leather thong was in Kioga's hand.

Now, while they ringed him enviously at re-spectful distance, the Snow Hawk dipped into bas-ket after basket, calmly sampling all that was good or sweet in Saki's bazaar—his proper right in the circumstances. . . .

All this transpired in the happier days before

Kioga, son of the first white civilized discoverer of this unknown strand, became the outlaw foreordained for future fame among the savage Shoni tribesmen. Yet even now no cronies had Kioga among these little redskins. He was The One Who Plays Alone, the pariah, the outcast. What friends he had were older folk—the river-men who took him everywhere in their great canoes, the aged ones who loved him for his sprightly walk and laughing face, and for little kindnesses he did, beyond the thought of the other wild children in primitive Hopeka-town.

One other loved him too—old Sawamic, Emperor-chief of the Seven Shoni tribes; for old Sawamic's lodge was without living son; and Kioga—body, heart and mind—was all and more than any warrior-chief could wish for in his own.

And now Sawamic came in person, to bring a fresh-killed buck to Saki of the single eye. Kioga put the buck into a wooden chest, out of the way of other things. Breathing hard from labor which he might have assigned to another, Sawamic still had time to speak a pleasant word with Kioga.

" 'Tis well you are returned, my son. Trouble brews among the warriors. Come soon to visit at my lodge again. 'Tis suitable a famous chief-to-be should learn to speak our several dialects."

"I will, Grandfather-chief, when Saki returns," promised Kioga, full of importance that so great a chief should speak to him in public before the other village boys.

Sawamic turned away. The band of Hopeka children followed, clinging to his robes. Through the dusk Kioga beheld a band of other figures, four warriors approaching with their heads together. Saluting him most respectfully to his face, when the old Emperor-chief had passed, the four stood looking after him, respect gone from their features, and hatred in its place.

Kioga saw. And seeing, he thought of what Saki had said, and Sawamic had confirmed, of hidden plottings against his rule among the Shoni. And so Kioga, instead of standing boldly forth and offering Saki's wares, as he had intended, raised the cover of the nearest wicker basket. Jumping quickly in, he lowered its top so that only a crack appeared. Through this he watched the oncoming warriors, led by Takaso.

Well Kioga knew this red-skinned malcontent who hailed from Sioket, a village far up-river. Leader among the secret Long-Knife society, Saki had said he was; and recalling that, Kioga eyed the nearing band the more closely as they came behind surly Takaso—tall, fierce, scarred on the jaw, and coldly truculent of gaze.

Nearing the bazaar, and observing its aged attendant nowhere in sight, the four paused, apparently to await Saki's return. But since she did not soon appear, the warriors squatted down and fell to talking. Deserted at the supper-hour, the bazaar was an ideal corner for exchanging confidences.

"You take great risks," said a lowered voice.

"Great ends demand great risks," said Takaso boldly, slapping his tomahawk with a lean brown hand. "And when Sawamic walks across the slippery log, we Long Knives will rise and rule the nation in his place. Men were given arms to wield weapons. Too long has Sawamic the Peacemaker held us back from plundering the rich villages of the People of the Plume upriver."

"*Aya!*" agreed another voice huskily. "But Sawamic's warriors suspect us; and they are many and quick to act."

"What matter if they do?" answered Takaso craftily. "They know not when we'll strike, nor whose will be the tomahawk."

"*Sssst!*" went some one warningly, at sound of a shambling step. "Silence! Saki returns."

"Ho, warriors!" cackled the old woman, shuffling into view. "What do you whisper of, hiding among my baskets, eh-eh?"

A companion nudged Takaso, pointing at a company of Sawamic's loyal stalwarts approaching through the dusk. The plotter started. It would do his cause no good to seem conspiring with others. Quickly, to allay suspicion—

"O Saki," he said in a loud voice calculated to carry to the ears of those approaching, "what will you trade for two canoes of redstone pipes, and eating-wares from far upriver—the finest to be had?"

Never lacking words where trading was involved, Saki answered swiftly: "Three baskets filled with feather robes." Then with an instinct which bade her to be sharp, she added: "But you must take them as they are, upon the spot."

Now this was trading sight unseen—but Sawamic's warriors were eying Takaso and he wished to look the part of a simple trader. He dared not hesitate.

"Agreed," he said loudly. "Here, warriors, take up these baskets. You, Teniko, and Arako, go fetch the pipes and wares from our canoes."

Nearer drew the group of loyal braves. The

eyes of all were sharply on this well-known fire-brand from another river-village.

Suddenly Saki voiced the query: "Where's Kioga?"

Almost Kioga answered from the depths of his basket. But just in time he checked himself. If he so much as spoke a word, it sealed his doom. Unsuspected bearer of Takaso's deadly secret, the merest hint of his presence within the basket would bring a killing stroke. More than that, if he betrayed himself, the beloved Sawamic's life was also forfeit. He must wait until the plotters had gone, then come forth and warn the Peacemaker.

But even with the thought, strong hands were laid upon the handles of the basket wherein he hid. It was raised and swung in time to the bearers' strides. He felt the container lowered grating on the river sands, and heard the liquid lap of water, the sounds of canoes being emptied and laden, the grunts of straining men at labor. He dared to raise the basket top a little, then lowered it without a sound. Takaso stood close beside him.

An instant more, again the feeling of being raised, then the gentle movement, up and down, made by a canoe rocking to the weight of a cargo. Once more Kioga peered forth. A warrior was shoving off. A weight fell down upon his creaking basket. He could see no more.

But Kioga felt the canoe turn upstream against the currents. He smelled the rich balsamic breath of the forest, bespeaking ferny jungle and trackless glade pressed only by the paws of prowling brutes. He sensed the rhythmic urging of the poles, and heard the *tump-a-tump* of a village drum dying to a whisper far behind. And finally, some miles north upon the silent river, he felt the long poles cease their rhythm, and heard the voice of Takaso.

"Now let us see if Saki robbed us," it said. Came then the sound of baskets being opened, and the rustle of feather robes pawed over in the torchlight. "All well in these," said Takaso. "Now we will open the last."

Another would have shrunk with fear. Not Kioga! As touch fell on the basket cover, he drew his knife with one hand, while with the other he pulled a robe down about his head. Takaso might find him here. But Takaso would never live to tell of it.

Up went the cover. Sinewy fingers clutched the topmost robe beneath which crouched the Snow Hawk, tight as a spring compressed. But suddenly came blood-stopping interruption—the jungle-jarring thunder of a tiger's voice. The basket cover fell.

Shrill yells of startled men. *Twang-twang-g-g* of bows discharging almost at Kioga's ear. Followed then the bite of frantically bending poles, the snarls of an angry animal receding with the shore, the taunts of the warriors at the wounded beast. Then once again the easy rhythm, the *swish-h-h* of curling water astern and the gurgle at the wooden prow.

Fears of having been out-traded were forgotten by the warriors in the greater dangers lurking along the river highway. For the moment Kioga was safe, scarce daring to swallow, lest his presence be discovered. Presently, however a wisp of down from the robe which hid him tickled his nostril and before he could help himself, he sneezed.

Again the poling rhythm stopped. He heard a whisper:

"What was that?"

He could sense the warriors straining all their ears. From ashore once more a forest denizen helped him. A wolf coughed, and howled hoarsely.

"T'yone has a cold," said Takaso as the tension eased. The canoe moved forward, and Kioga's heart took up its beat again. The green-walled forest glided past the hurrying craft. Copper shades of men dipped wetly gleaming rods of silver into sepia water. Without pause the Shoni warriors labored hour after hour, until at last with a grunt of satisfaction Takaso spoke.

"The village of Sioket—just around the bend. I see a light upon the wall. We'll trade these furs with that old bag of bones K'yopit, and pass the word about among our secret brethren that Sawamic's skull is to be cloven."

"K'yopit is coming now," declared Teniko.

"Old fox! He smells a trade ten sleeps away," grumbled Takaso. And then in louder tones: "*A-hai*, Wrinkle-belly, keeper of Sioket's captive wolves! Three baskets of feather robes from Hopeka. What will you give for them?"

"First I must look at each and every one," whined old K'yopit. "I'm very poor, *eya*, and the skins from Hopeka are not what they used to be."

K'yopit's canoe touched against the greater trading-craft. Nimble as a wizened monkey, he climbed to the higher level, dwarfed among the tall straight warriors. From one basket he dragged out all the magnificent gleaming robes.

"*Bah-bah!* What mangy skins!" muttered the old red Shylock craftily. "They're hardly worth the wearing."

"The best Hopeka boasts, you dry-skinned skeleton!" retorted Takaso, on a note of indignation. "Ten hunting-jackets, worked in stained quills, will take three baskets full."

"Ten jackets!" cried K'yopit jeeringly, diving into the second basket and clawing forth all its contents. "You must be mad. I'd give but four for all I've seen thus far."

K'yopit's skinny fingers raised the cover of the third basket, fumbling with the skin. Kioga felt dry hooks close about his ear and waited tensely for discovery. He felt K'yopit start in deep amazement as he explored Kioga's features with his fingers.

"Eight, then—give us eight jackets and we'll have done," Takaso was saying.

"A skin worth having!" reflected K'yopit as his hand paused upon Kioga's neck. "A slave escaping—and Takaso does not know of it." He shut down the lid upon Kioga with a bang. "Say five jackets," he announced, "and I will trade. Five jackets—beaded front and back with colored shells, and hung with soft long fringe, that make the maidens turn and look. Take five."

Takaso wavered; and seeing it, K'yopit eyed him with a quick shrewd glance. "Six I might give," he added suddenly, "if you bear the baskets to my lodge. Ask more—and throw them in the river!"

"Six beaded jackets I will take," agreed Takaso at last, "Where are the jackets?"

"At my lodge," answered the other, binding the covers of his baskets securely with lengths of leather thong. "Deliver the baskets thither, and the jackets shall be yours."

And thus, without more ado, it was done. Takaso and his warriors took the fruits of their trade and went about other affairs in the upriver village.

In the lodge of K'yopit, when they had gone, the old redskin turned to the third basket, untied the thong, threw back the cover, and seizing Kioga by the hair, raised him into view.

Half suffocated by the closing of the basket and the muffling robe, Kioga was in no condition to resist. Before his strength returned, K'yopit relieved him of his knife and tied his wrists behind him.

"Six buckskin jackets—little enough for one so lean and strong," muttered old K'yopit, feeling of Kioga's lithe young muscles. "You'll be a fine slave to bear my water and guard my lodge."

Now slavery (uncommon among American Indians except in the Pacific Northwest) among the Shoni is of this nature: Whoso counts *coup* upon an enemy in open battle, or during raids upon another village, declaring his intention, may take his captive as a slave, no matter what the captive's age. Often captivity becomes in fact adoption; and many well-fed slaves there be among the Seven Tribes who would not exchange these light shackles for their former way of life. When a slave seeks escape, Shoni primal law has always held that whoso captures him becomes his owner. If the captor so desires, he may trade him back to his previous owner for what he can obtain, or else support him.

A slave in Hopeka this youth must have been, thought K'yopit—else why had he been seeking to escape? Right glad was the old trader to acquire this strong young property to do the labors which long had been wearisome to him.

"You'll help me feed the captive wolves," went on K'yopit, rubbing his hands with satisfaction.

From somewhere near there came a mournful sound, howled up from a savage throat among K'yopit's ferocious charges. These were the totem beasts of Sioket village. Penned in a log-walled den just outside the palisade, the wolves were fed but twice a week in order that their hunger-howls might frighten off all river-spirits—a superstitious custom ancient as the people who believed in it.

"To feed the wolves—there is no shame in that. But—I—a slave?" thought the aghast Snow Hawk, with dilating pupils. "I,—Kioga,—a water-bearer to this old scalp atop a skeleton!"

"Why not—or would you have me tell the warriors you are here?" cackled the old savage, divining Kioga's thoughts. But Kioga's face presented the blankness of a wall.

"Tell them—or not," he said with a show of indifference. "Who then would be your slave?"

"You are a clever youth," K'yopit grinned.

"Clever," conceded Kioga, "—and hungry as well."

"Eh! Already?"

"Even a slave must eat," said Kioga pointedly, "if he is to remain useful to his master."

"That's true," said old K'yopit grudgingly. Going to one of the baskets, wherein he kept meat for the fierce communal pets, he took up a chunk of meat and flung it before the Snow Hawk. "Sweet juicy venison to make thee strong. Eat!"

Kioga eyed the meat. "Cut my cords that I may obey," he said. Warily K'yopit loosened the thongs a trifle, and Kioga took up the meat. "Such a little piece—and stale," he said indignantly and threw it in a corner. A cooking-pot was bubbling near by. Into this Kioga reached, and fishing up a tender fowl, devoured it in twenty mouthfuls.

The old red miser's eyes were fairly popping. "You'll eat me out of lodge and home!" he cried.

"Ah, *bah!*" said Kioga. "I am growing—not like thee, old Rattle-bones, who only shrink with age."

" 'Tis true," agreed K'yopit mournfully. He began to wonder if after all he had had the better of his trade with Takaso. When Kioga had eaten, again K'yopit tightened his bonds.

Elsewhere in Sioket, Takaso paced the lodge of a friend restlessly. "It seems to me," he said, time and again, "K'yopit acted very strangely—in that he offered four and finally gave up six hunting shirts for our three baskets. This is most strange. I cannot understand it."

His two companions of the river episode smoked lazily, indifferently. When presently Takaso left the lodge, Teniko laughed.

"Uneasy are the covetous. When they gain much, they would gain more. When more they gain, 'tis not enough."

But Takaso, far from being covetous, was in truth, uneasy. Suspicious by nature, K'yopit's peculiar actions had unsettled him, filled him with a vague but troublous apprehension that drove him toward the trader's lodge to reconnoiter.

Slowly he neared K'yopit's hovel, muffled to the eyes in his blanket; glancing about to see that none were near, he moved into its shadow. And thus Takaso overheard part of the talk between K'yopit and another, at sound of whose voice Takaso started.

With his knife's sharp edge Takaso warily cut through a barken patch on the dilapidated lodge, and peered within. His worst fears were realized. He suddenly recalled that sneeze, back somewhere along the river, and that not he nor any of his warriors had looked into that third basket, which now stood empty and open in a corner. He remembered Saki's missing Kioga. And he realized that Kioga had been concealed in that third basket and must have heard their plot against the Emperor-chief.

Takaso's eyes narrowed. He gripped his tomahawk in hand, then belted it again. The village was no place for a killing. K'yopit was moving toward the exit and passing through, leaving Kioga squatting by the fire, looking at his tied hands. K'yopit had not gone ten paces before Takaso stepped from the shadows to his side.

"*Ai*, Wrinkle-belly, I see the reason for your eagerness to trade with us!"

K'yopit shrank back guiltily, then recovered. "The more fool you, seeing too late what cannot now be altered," he answered boldly.

"I want the boy myself," said Takaso, himself the pleader now. "I knew not he was in that basket. Indeed, his father is my closest friend, a great warrior in Hopeka-town."

"Eh-eh?" demanded K'yopit. "But I thought—" There he checked himself in time, and continued on another line to cover his momentary confusion. "Worthy Takaso!" he said ironically. "Surely since it is for a bosom friend, you will pay me a fine high price for him."

"Ask what you will," answered Takaso sullenly.

"Ask what I will!" thought K'yopit, confused more deeply still: for if Kioga were no slave, as first he had surmised, Takaso had but to demand that he be set at liberty. Who—least of all trembling old K'yopit—would dare detain him then? But trading whets the wits. K'yopit reasoned: "The treacherous of heart do not develop friendships overnight. Takaso has some cause to fear the boy—else why this open offer for one who is no slave at all?" Then seeing Takaso impatient: "Twenty prime snow-leopard pelts," he demanded on a bold impulse.

"I'll give fifteen," answered Takaso, prepared to give three times as many, if only that secret Kioga shared could be confined to him alone.

"He'll give fifteen," thought K'yopit, to himself again. "He wants him very badly, then. Eh-eh, there's something here I do not understand. But better that I wash my hands of it while still there's time. If this should be a chieftain's kin—" K'yopit shivered slightly. But to Takaso he turned a face of adamant: "Twenty pelts—not one skin less, or I will keep him!"

"Then twenty let it be," said Takaso with a false show of rage. "But where will I get twenty pelts this night?"

"Twenty pelts, delivered at my door," cackled the inexorable K'yopit, like cat that plays with mouse, "or mayhap I'll send the boy back to Hopeka myself."

Even K'yopit was amazed at the effect of this blind random threat. Takaso paled, then gained command of himself again, and looked daggers at the little wizened trader. "Then I will arrange down at the river-front to get the skins. But look you, Wrinkle-belly: No one must see me take him away. You understand?"

"Better than you think," reflected K'yopit, while aloud he answered: "*Ai-yah!* Not even I shall see you go. I'll bind his mouth and put him in a basket as he came. I'll mark it with a turkey plume hung on the handle. I wish to know no more of this. Therefore I will go away before you come."

Within the lodge Kioga crouched bound and helpless, with ear pressed listening to the wall.

K'yopit entered. "*N-nyi,*" he whined with a show of apprehension. "Crawl back into the basket. The warriors who brought you here are coming back. Quick, or you will be discovered," urged the old man, holding something hid behind his back.

Affecting haste and fear, Kioga obeyed. With a sudden movement K'yopit bound his mouth up tightly. Kioga did not resist; the hour was not ripe to do so. When the time came he would sell his life as wildcats do. Until then he husbanded his strength. K'yopit secured the fastenings of the basket cover, and marked it as agreed. Then K'yopit shuffled from the lodge and left the door-skin flap hang open.

Silently, with utmost patience, Kioga set to work within his prison. Of his sharp strong teeth he now had urgent need. With slowly numbing fingers he worked to get that gag of skin from between his jaws. Long minutes, picking at K'yopit's knots, resulted in success. Now, wrists at teeth, he gnawed his rawhide bonds, and in the end his hands were also free, the thong preserved against some future need. Then flexing his wrists, he tried his strength against the heavy basket. With time, perhaps, he had broken out, for his was a muscular strength rarely given to one so young. But suddenly he ceased all effort, listening.

Takaso came, in company of Teniko. Kioga heard them moving in the darkened lodge, toward his basket; and at once he replaced the gag against the time when Takaso would undoubtedly look in upon him.

"The feather marker," whispered Teniko. "This is the one."

"Make sure," hissed Takaso. "Reach in and feel if his mouth is stopped. One cannot see in such darkness so thick as is this!"

Up went the cover. Sinewy fingers ascertained that the gag still performed its office. "A knife-thrust would better silence him," said Teniko grimly through his teeth.

"And leave a trail of blood as well," warned Takaso swiftly, shutting down the lid again securely. "I know of twenty better ways to still a tongue. Of all of them the river is the best. Quick, now, take up your side and let us go."

Again Kioga knew the sensation of being lifted, but now there was no uncertainty as to his fate. Yet still he waited, ready but relaxed, silent, alert as a ferret—excited, truly, but without a trace of panic.

He felt cool outer air blow through the interstices of his reedy cell and drew away the gag.

They neared the gate; the sentry there would challenge, inquire perhaps into the contents of the basket. But that was pure formality in time of peace, the loosest kind of primitive customs inspection. But to cry out were folly, with those sharp tomahawks so near and ready.

"Ho, warriors!" a voice called. "What have you in that basket?"

"The best of old K'yopit's skins," replied Takaso boldly. "And dearly have they cost me!"

The sentry laughed. "Whoever gets K'yopit's best at any price deserves it. I wish you good of it. Pass, warriors. Make haste. We throw the plumstones—I am winning."

Kioga heard a creak. The gates swung wide. The warriors passed out. At sound of passing footsteps, the totem wolves, denned in their enclosure just outside the village gate, began to snap and snarl and then gave famished tongue. And if Kioga's flesh began to creep, there was an excellent reason.

For these are the fiercest wolves on earth—not wolves such as are seen in park and steel-barred zoo, but wolves of far Nato'wa, related to the Dire wolves of deep antiquity; tall as Great Danes at the shoulder, with fangs like keen stilettos.

Ravenous, with bellies knotted up by long denial, their howling hunger clamored up. Grating scratches on the wall bespoke the fury with which they moved along with Takaso and Teniko, no more than that high log wall of their enclosure between.

And suddenly Takaso spoke. "*Ahu!* Of all the twenty ways to rid ourselves of Kioga, the twenty-first is best."

"What's in your mind?" asked Teniko as they lowered the basket between them. "To sink him in a whirlpool with a stone tied to the handle?"

"The river often gives up its dead," Takaso answered; "but when the jaws of Soiket's wolves devour, there's nothing left to be returned."

Within his cell Kioga's blood ran cold. He heard the wolves increase their din, expectant of some offering from without. And then Kioga of the fearless heart had to grip his courage tight in both his hands: To die in the night beneath such yellow fangs!

"A great idea!" said Teniko. "Quick, then, and have an end of it!" And with the words he loosened the cover of the basket.

Kioga heard them grunt, as with a mighty effort they raised the basket atop the wall. A moment more, and they would overturn it and dump him out to be bitten and butchered. And then, too late, Kioga gave the wild shrill yell he hitherto had stifled.

Maddened by the familiar sound of a basket on the wall, the wolves raised up a fiendish din which drowned his one voice out. In desperation Kioga kicked mightily, clinging the while to avoid being hurled down those yelling throats. What with his struggles and the awkwardness of the basket so high above their heads, Takaso and his friend lost both their holds upon it.

Kioga fell groundward, still contained within his prison. But that prison proved a godsend now. For luckily the reed frame held together. Its cover flapping open, upside-down the basket fell, covering Kioga.

Rendered helpless for the moment by his heavy fall, Kioga let one hand protrude, and jerked it in just as a gaunt-jawed wolf made snap for it—but not before one fang had ripped his palm.

A dozen fierce hot breaths beat through the baffling wicker-work, inside of which Kioga crouched, aware of his good fortune and seeking means of utilizing it. Through a hole stove in one corner by the fall, he could dimly see the wall near by. Toward this he edged the basket, inch by inch, by raising it a little and pushing forward.

But as he went, strong jaws tore at the stout vine tendrils of which it was woven. One brute ripped out a section large enough to get his head half in. And in that moment Kioga had his golden inspiration.

The basket—now a cage—was at the wall. An old gray pointed head jammed snarling through the opening, maddened by the smell of Kioga's blood. Quick as a flash Kioga snapped a running noose, made of the cords which once had bound him, about its snout, drew it tight to close the jaws, and made a knot. Then with both hands—enduring the agony of using the one which had been bitten—he seized it by the windpipe. A moment passed—another, before the wolf gave up its thrashing and stretched out senseless.

Kioga thrust the wolf's head, smeared with his own blood, out among its ravening fellows. And at once their raving ceased. There was the tear of flesh, the crunch of bone, a hideous worrying: the totem pack was feeding on part of itself, with the basket and the one beneath it overlooked.

This was the moment for which Kioga had

hoped. When it seemed that all the wolves were occupied, with one quick thrust he hurled his cage among them. Then, as a spring of steel recoils, Kioga leaped straight upward into air. All of the agility and quickness gained in years of forest roving was in that quick release of energy. Had he been less swift, the nearest wolf had pulled him down. Instead it got no more than half his loincloth. And had he fallen back, the other long hard-snapping jaws had chopped him into bits. But Kioga did not fall back.

He grasped, instead, the top rim of the den-wall, near the narrow gate, and hung there just beyond the reach of slavering jaws. Beyond the den-wall Takaso would have looked to make certain that Kioga was dragged down to death, but for a sudden startling diversion. Even as the basket had crashed amid the dens, a short but infuriated figure in a tattered blanket rushed from the village and sprang among them, crying malediction. It was K'yopit the trader, who had spied upon them from the village wall, roused to a fury of righteous anger at them who would destroy a child so inhumanly.

But K'yopit's ninety years could not long support his anger. That white blaze flickered swiftly out. When Kioga looked first above the wolf-den wall, the trader's other self had just returned, and suddenly K'yopit wheeled and ran like rat before the terriers.

Behind, with knives and clubs uplifted, the warriors pursued fiercely, to avenge his interference. Straight past the dens K'yopit scurried, bleating in fear of death. Kioga saw the old features contorted with the agony of running. And though Kioga knew him for a rascal, he none the less was filled with pity for a helpless old man.

K'yopit stumbled past the gateway to the dens, but did not see Kioga. Takaso and his warriors glimpsed the boy a-perch upon the wall beside the wolf-den gate. Takaso's hand shot forward— *thud!*—his knife was quivering in the wall beside Kioga's hand.

Swiftly Kioga dropped to earth outside the dens. The plotters now were closing in. To the gate Kioga darted, threw up its bar, and swung it wide before they could divine his intention.

Out with a rush like water from a bursting dam two dozen shaggy giant bodies charged. The village totem wolves were freed! In panic Takaso and the others broke pursuit before that snarling white display of fangs, and ran toward their canoe, the loud-tonguing pack close on their heels.

Seizing a lance that Teniko had dropped in his amazement, Kioga melted into the thickets, glancing back to watch the outcome of his ruse. The totem wolves proved but a momentary threat. With freedom offering, the pack was racing off into the forest.

K'yopit lay exhausted on the sand. Takaso stood above him, his tomahawk bared. The others watched from their canoe.

"Whither went the boy?" demanded Takaso savagely. "Answer, quick, before I slice thine ears off!"

"I do not know—I do not know," protested the terror-stricken old trader. Cowering pitifully, K'yopit wrapped his arms about Takaso's knees and begged for life—in vain. He looked toward the shore—no escape in that direction. Up went the shining tomahawk. Then—

Whis-s-s-k!

Soft as breath of air a slim spear came singing, skewering the tomahawk arm through the biceps. Takaso yelled in surprise and pain and warning, pointing toward the forest whence the spear had come.

"Ashore! Ashore—the Snow Hawk—get him!"

Quick to obey, his companions forced the canoe's hard prow against the bank and plunged into the looming forest, while K'yopit's aged feet grew wings, and he was seen no more.

The Shoni mingle caution with their bravery. They do not wander by choice in the deeper glades where leopards prowl and tigers lair. The friends of Takaso came quickly forth.

"He's gone," they said. "He'll fill a tiger's belly."

Takaso broke the spear and wrapped a strip of hide about his arm by way of bandage. "Your words are empty as your heads. Know you not he roams abroad with bears and beasts while all the villages are asleep? I shall not paddle for a month. But waste no time, you others. Back to the village! Pass the word among our allies to arrow him on sight. While Kioga lives, our scalps are all in danger."

Spurred by a common fear of betrayal to Sawamic, whose life they plotted, the warriors plunged deep their poles and sent the trade-canoe furiously forward. And in the forest Kioga fled as never in his life before, toward Hopeka.

The race was on—his speed of hand and foot, his stamina, against the strength of these warriors, aided by the river-currents. The race, for all its evident one-sidedness, offered slight advantage to either. For where the river made wide turns and bends, Kioga gained by traveling a straighter course; and where the stream was straight, the trade-canoe cut down his earlier lead.

Upon the river hazards waited. But the place of every sunken rock and treacherous cross-rip was charted upon the brains of the river-men and easily evaded. In the forest through which Kioga fled, the barriers were infinitely more frequent.

Here a great tree twelve feet in diameter, had fallen on the path. Straight at it Kioga rushed, sprang halfway up, found purchase on its deep-grooved bark and scrambled atop it. Then down to its far side he lightly leaped—squarely upon a puma, licking fresh bones to whiteness with its red, barbed tongue. But boy and startled puma at once broke apart, each fleeing, though for different reasons.

But the incident threw Kioga off his stride. A ground-vine completed his downfall. He picked himself up, an old ache in his lower leg, and staggered on to where the gleaming river abutted on the trail he followed.

In view upstream the canoe of Takaso was coming swiftly, white bone in teeth. Lamed by his fall, Kioga could not now outpace that flying craft. But there were other ways. . . .

Not far ahead white water roared about a rapid which this deep craft could not negotiate, he knew. If pass it would, it must come close to shore, where smoother water ran, below a scarp of overhanging granite. Upon that scarp Kioga quickly rolled two great round boulders.

The trade-canoe turned shoreward, the pole-men intent upon the treacherous eddies. Takaso, with his one good hand, steered astern. A moment, waiting, Kioga crouched. The long canoe came nearer; its prow was not yet below him, when he pushed over the first boulder. Caroming from a stony spur, it spun away and did no damage.

The second poised, this time Kioga stood erect, exposed to the arrows of the shouting warriors. A quick shaft whistled past his head, another between his legs. With infinite care Kioga waited, aimed, let fall. The stone dropped hissing, and bomb-like struck amidships. Black water rushed in through the hole it made. A hundred feet down-river the canoe foundered, far offshore.

Kioga hurried on; Hopeka now not many miles away—Hopeka-town where old Sawamic the Emperor-chief slept, unconscious of the drama now enacting with his life the forfeit if Kioga's strength gave out. For with their hand forced, the enemies must needs strike at once.

Yet Takaso and his warriors were not defeated. Kioga had the start of them; but where, once ashore, they ran, he limped more slowly on his way. But as he went Kioga knew a little thrill of satisfaction. Not far ahead—unless some prowling brute had sprung it—was the runway snare which he and Ohali had made and set the other day.

With eyes upon the lookout, he presently saw it—undisturbed. He leaped the outspread lurking noose. His quick ear heard the sound of his pursuers. With head turned halfway backward he listened to determine if the snare would act.

Coming at full speed along the trail Takaso overleaped the waiting noose and saw it not. Not so the unlucky Teniko, who tripped it cleanly. He sprawled, but halfway to the ground Kioga's

springe acted. The other warriors close behind him
sent up a yell, whereat Kioga, hearing, grinned.

There was a leafy commotion just beside the
trail, then the upward thrash of a limber sapling.
Takaso wheeled to see a startling sight—Teniko
soaring upward into air like trout on giant's fish-
ing-rod. An instant in midair he hung head-down-
ward, caught about one ankle. Then with a snap
one of Kioga's knots slipped open. Twisting
toward the ground, Teniko dropped, all flying
arms and legs, to land with a sickening thud
among his friends—and lie inert.

From far ahead a defiant laugh rang back.

Takaso looked into the eyes of his remaining
warriors, with something closely kin to awe. But
greater than their awe was fear of imminent
disclosure. Once more the warriors took up the
pursuit. But now they went more carefully, less
hastily.

And so Kioga dragged himself just before them
to Hopeka-town, a strange and bloody limping figure who scarce had passed between the closing
gates when Takaso and his warriors arrived, de-
manding admission. There was a momentary
delay, while they identified themselves.

Swift thoughts raced through Kioga's head. Far
gone in exhaustion as now he was, the distance to
Sawamic's lodge seemed doubly long. If the pursu-
ing warriors found him ere he reached it, they
would most surely tomahawk him, inventing pretext for their act. The fastenings of the gate were
grating behind him. Takaso and his companions
were being admitted.

With his last strength Kioga turned another
way, his wits still functioning—straight for the ba-

zaar of old Saki, who drew in hissing breath as he came near.

"You bleed and pant! What's happened you? Where have you been?"

"Quick, Saki!" he gasped. "Hide me—*hide me!*"

Catching that note of desperate urgency, the old woman rose, drew back a robe that hung rug-like from a horizontal pole. A dark place offered. "In here," she whispered, and in Kioga threw himself. Upon the earth old Saki perched, owl-like and imperturbable, just as Takaso walked swiftly near, a question in his mouhh.

"Hast seen the youth Kioga, old witch?" he demanded. Kioga heard Saki answer vaguely:

"What do you want of him, O Double-Tongue?"

Curbing his impatience, Takaso answered: "I wish to give him this long sharp knife."

"He went toward Sawamic's lodge, limping and bloody. If you hurry, you may catch up with him," said Saki.

Kioga heard the footfalls of Takaso die away ere Saki came to him to bathe his wounded hand. All was lost, he thought, unless—

There was one thing which would reach and warn Sawamic before Takaso arrived. In a rush of words he told old Saki all. Then:

"Cry out, Grandmother! Cry out in thy mighty voice, or Sawamic will be a dead chieftain."

And cry out Saki did, in strident, piercing tones that fairly shook the village.

"*Ohai! Ohai!* One goes to kill Sawamic! To arms, you warriors! Defend your chief! *Ohai*, Peacemaker, beware the arrow from behind! Death to all traitors!"

Now rose a sudden bedlam between the high

log walls. Takaso, already creeping through the door of Sawamic's darkened lodge, caught the rising swell of it, hesitated for one fatal moment, then hurled his tomahawk at a reclining figure and wheeled to make his escape.

But he was too late!

As he burst into the open a ring of warriors hemmed him in, with bending bows. There was no fight. It was an execution, quick and bloody. Takaso fell with twenty arrows through his body before old Sawamic appeared behind him at the doorway, a slight scratch, no more, upon his brow.

But in Saki's bazaar, four lean avenging shadows suddenly appeared, with knives and hatchets baring. The companions of Takaso, hearing her outcry, had divined the reason. Hurling the shrieking old woman from her perch atop a chest, and raising up the cover, they drove in their spears at something huddled up within it—the last act of their mortal lives. For as they wheeled to number Saki among their slain, a storm of arrows carried death among them, riddling them with the barbs of Sawamic's faithful.

A moment later the old Emperor-chief of all the Seven Shoni tribes drew near, encircled by a band of his closest retainers, informing him of all that had just transpired.

A little speechless group, among them Saki, had gathered round an open chest, and gazed down into it. The group fell back, all save old Saki, upon whose withered cheek great tears were glistening below her single eye.

Sawamic paused beside the open chest from which the rigid spears protruded. Sawamic's eye grew dim, and something in his strong old spirit seemed to crumble at thought of Kioga's laughter, nevermore to echo throughout his lodge.

"Weep not, Saki," he said in kindly tones, placing a sympathetic hand upon her shaking shoulder. The shaking ceased. Then Saki was convulsed again before she spoke.

"Weep—do I seem to weep? Not so, O Chief. I laugh. For they have only killed the dead. Look closer. 'Tis a deer they've speared to earth—the buck you sent me—a buck these many hours dead."

"Where, then, is Kioga?" cried Sawamic, his seamed face changing as if the sun were rising up behind his eyes.

"I'm almost sitting on him," cried Saki, rising from before her rack of robes and drawing one aside, that Sawamic might gaze within. "I fended them from that chest which held the buck you sent this morning. And they—the simple fools— thrust in their spears. Before they knew the truth—*eh-hee*—your warriors shot them down."

"*Hai-ya*, Kioga," called the near-sighted old chief to the lad who lay curled up and breathing heavily upon the ground. "Come forth, that we may honor thee. Come forth, I say—"

"*Ssst!* Be quiet!" said Saki, suddenly, forgetful of the quality of him to whom she spoke. Then like a troubled old hen she drove Sawamic and all the rest before her. "Away—away with all of you," she said in bated tones. "Kioga is asleep."

PART III

Unharmed, He Dwelt Among the Forest People

The Snow Hawk, called by the Shoni folk Kioga, retired from the village of Hopeka in some haste, yet certainly not fast enough to sate the wrath of three termagant squaws who chased him to the gate, reviling every step. But at the gate they paused, while he fled on—out into the fierce unconquered wilderness his white parents had discovered in the Arctic—a volcano-warmed region only lately known to civilized men.

The cause of his precipitate departure was a captive yearling bear, Kioga's favorite pet, unwittingly admitted to a storage lodge. What happened there is still a cause for merriment in Hopeka: The bear went in thin and came out round as a Shoni signal drum. And since this was the third occasion of the sort, quite naturally the squaws gave way to anger; and Kioga, in his turn, to shrewd retreat.

Whereas to all the other red-skinned children, Hopeka-town was sanctuary, for Kioga to flee out into the forest was typical. For in the forest—as every Shoni old enough to speak could tell—Kioga had a host of friends. Of these none were more dear to him than the troops of shaggy bears who roamed the virgin timberlands some leagues distant from Hopeka.

Now, as ever in the past, it was these friendly beasts Kioga sought, before the first storm of the season broke. In seeking them he found another—but of that other, more in its place. . . .

Through an old and hoary forest rooted along the sloping shoulder of a northern mountainside, a winter gale blew moaning, spewing frigid diamond-dust in hissing clouds upon deep drifts of snow already crusted with the glaze of freezing weather.

Once, through the dimness of the blizzard, a lone lean skulking form came floating past, thick brush between hindlegs—a gaunt old solitary wolf, the very grayish ghost of wintry loneliness. Even as he went, his trail was covered, his scent obliterated. And a moment later, a young spike-buck passing by took no alarm until white bayonets were shearing his jugular.

Dead in his tracks the spike-buck fell quivering: and instantly the wolf crouched beside him, tearing out great chunks of flesh. . . . Already the buck's red lolling tongue was freezing. About the two prone forms the driving icy crystals were piling up, effacing carmine spots, concealing the grim marks of wilderness tragedy.

Gorging on the fat and tender venison until his shaggy sides were swelling, the old gray killer heard no sound beyond the savage crunch of bones between his teeth. But up along the trail T'yone earlier had used, two other shadows now came silently. Of these, one was feline, close to the ground, with a round furry tail that made its length a good eleven feet. Its eyes were burning beryls.

The other shade belonged not in this wintry scene of savagery; yet somehow, after second glance, did belong. For as the puma crouched, thus also crouched the man-cub, so close beside the brute that the coats of thick warm fur, in which their bodies were enclosed, touched. They somehow looked alike, both lean and lithe and supple. The fur capote with which the man-cub's garb was capped, fell back behind his neck. His tangled thatch of raven hair, powdered through with gems of sparkling snow, tossed unruly in the tearing winds, and stung his lean brown cheeks.

From green-blazing eyes no whit less fierce than those which burned on a lower level beside him, Kioga the Snow Hawk intently watched that little hillock on the trail ahead. And in the handsome dark-skinned face a light of understanding broke.

"Ho, Mika!" he breathed to that lean, grinning panther at his side. "T'yone leaped before us—for I hear a leg-bone crunched! But I am empty— yah!—just like a bullock's horn. No wolf will rob me of my meat, *ehu!* Not while my leather snake is close at hand!"

And with the whispered words Kioga took from round his waist a plaited tapered hide lash and flicked it flat behind him. Then—*ssss-whack!*—he whipped it sharply forth against the hillock. Up with a snarl bounded the old lone wolf, baring bloody fangs at this strange pair who faced him down the trail.

"*Hai,* Crack-bone! Quick—away with you!" cried the Snow Hawk, moving forward two quick paces and staking all on one good bluster.

But here was one not thus simply to be fronted down. Close against the snow the old lone crouching killer held his vulnerable throat, and circled half around his fallen prey in search of better foothold.

Once more the leather thong came slashing forth and drew his blood behind the shoulder. Then old T'yone, two hundred pounds of bone and leathery sinew, and lightning-quick for all his years, came rushing fire-eyed upon the Snow Hawk, his ruse in this attack an old and subtle one. For as he came, the great wolf slashed not at the throat, as is the custom of his breed, but chopped instead with deadly ferocity lower down—a snap that must have cut Kioga's knee-pan cleanly out.

But if T'yone was quick, Kioga was the quicker by the fraction of a second. There was no tear of flesh and gristle. Instead a hollow traplike clash foretold T'yone's miss. Nor had he second chance to snap again.

A steely grip concealed in gloves of buckskin clamped quickly round those jaws just as they closed. Legs like links of iron chain closed tightly round his flanks—all in that little moment before T'yone could come erect from his rush.

With sudden movement of the wrist Kioga cast two half-hitches of his leather lash about the wolf's long jaws. Unscabbarding, he plunged his thin bone knife deep into the shaggy chest, severing the great blood vessels with two rapid thrusts, and leaping clear. And as he sprang away, Mika rushed in belatedly, then drew away, to watch T'yone die.

T'yone still bit the snow in his death-paroxysm when Kioga and his snarling consort were in their turn crouching at the new-killed spike-buck. Without a pause they ate, Mika the puma shearing off great pieces with his side-jaw teeth, Kioga severing juicy steaming slices with his knife and wolfing them down in the need to fill his famished belly, empty these three long hungry days. They ate incredible quantities, as hungry meat-eaters always do, and then ate more for fuller measure. And having swallowed all they could contain, both looked together for a warm place in which to digest their meal in comfort.

Luck held. Kioga, probing with a tree-branch, broke through a thin crust of ice, to find an empty cave; into this they disappeared, the man-cub first, the puma slinking slowly after. And though a clinging scent told them they had preempted the former home of a bear, they gave the fact but little thought. Presently their trail filled up with snow. No one, not having seen them enter, could have known that two wild creatures had denned up there.

Strengthened by the fresh meat, Kioga felt about him in the darkness and raked together a heap of leaves and trash. On this he threw himself to rest. Soon the panther, having investigated each corner of the ancient lair, returned and stretched beside him. Upon the warm and silken side Kioga laid his head.

Without, the cold winds howled and muttered eerily. The great trees cracked and groaned, straining at their anchoring roots and bowing in homage to the winter storm, like subject warriors armored in ice. Within, drawn closer by the need for common warmth, Mika and Kioga fell asleep.

Six hours passed before they stirred. Then neither could have told what brought his head erect, with listening ears and muscles tensed by strange suspense. Beyond the entrance to the den the winds were muttering still, and crystal snow still hissed to earth. These sounds had not awakened them. Some other new, extraneous note had broken through their slumbers.

It came again. A thin yet piercing cry, not brute, but human, threaded through the moan of the winds. Hard on its terror-note, there came the voice of fiercest hunger ravening through the night.

"T'yone and his brother-wolves are on the run," Kioga said with a curl of the lip that told his hatred of the pack.

Too long had he roamed beyond the walls of the primitive village that was his sometime home not to know the meaning of those sounds. Somewhere out in the dark of night the panting pack was closing in. Somewhere a hunted creature—a human creature like himself—stood back to tree, with pounding heart and fear-dilated eyes. Ever closer came a ring of shining double disks, and fangs that dripped with hot saliva whetted and champed together. Then, suddenly—could that be human scream, so frantic, so wild with terror? Silence put a stop to it. The pack was feeding. The end had come.

Mika's savage head dropped back contentedly. Too late, Kioga thought, for him to offer aid. He also sought oblivion. He laid his head upon the puma's side and heard it purring like the stone with which the Shoni women ground up berry-pits. But sleep would not return. Out in that stormy darkness one of his own kind had perished.

The timbre of the voice still puzzled him. Then with a start, he realized. No man's scream that last one, but a woman's.

With a cry that was half-sob, he sprang up with a bound. Had not Awena, his Indian foster-mother, gone to visit in another village before the rivers froze? The chance was remote—and yet, it could have been her voice that he had heard.

Outside the den, the winds howled louder. A skin of ice had formed upon the wall of snow which sealed the cave—condensing moisture from the lungs of those who lay within. Without a pause Kioga smashed it through and moved alone into the storm, armed with his whip.

The icy snow slashed down like buckshot. The faintest light from moon and northern lights high up above the storm relieved the gloom of open spaces. But elsewhere the forest loomed blackly.

How, out amid that screeching chaos, would he find the scene of forest tragedy? Wolflike, he gave the answer by his acts, first circling to get the wind from every quarter in his nostrils. The place could not be farther than the span which human voice could carry through the noises of this night. Then—ah!—two-thirds about the ring, Kioga stiffened. Blown by the north wind close against the earth, the strong wolf-smell was in his nose. A moment leaning low against the storm before he heard the yap and snarling of the pack, with now and then the crack of splintering bone in jaws of iron.

The awful sounds came from a deep ravine all overhung with leaning evergreens. Whip in hand, Kioga warily neared, raising up the snow-hung boughs and passing quietly beneath. The acrid stench of wolves came evilly, and with it the smell of blood, fresh-let, the air still warm with it. Parting the branches on the lip of the ravine, Kioga looked downward into a little open space, wherein one tree stood solitary. The vague auroral light intensified, lighting up the scene in ghastly green and silver.

A dozen of this earth's most savage life-destroyers crouched feeding on new-killed prey. Ears laid back and fangs displayed, each tore off a share, retreating snarling to consume its grisly portion.

With anxious eyes upon the dead, Kioga loosed a sigh of deep relief. That poor unlucky thing below those crouching forms had not been Awena. The copper band about the hair marked the victim as of another tribe.

All this he noted in the briefest instant—then something else which made him start: Two of the pack, both lesser brutes not yet full-grown, and driven by the others from the feast, leaped up and down in most peculiar fashion. Observing them, Kioga soon glimpsed the thing at which they sprang.

Swinging, swaying, dipping from a long evergreen bough, it was a cradle-board, hung by its thongs almost within the reach of snapping jaws, had not the howling winds tossed up and down the branch from which it dangled. Within its wrappings would be a child, saved by the last act of a devoted mother.

Time and again the young wolves sprang to seize the dangling prey, and each time fell a little short. But presently one of the older feeders rose, licking his chops, and snarled the young pair aside. Then with a single leap, straight up he rose, above the level of the bough. His white-steam breath blew on the infant's face; his great jaws clamped upon the cradle-board.

But before the force of gravity could pull both down into the red-stained snow, a writhing snake-like thing came darting forth, and with a smart resounding *crack* drew blood from the leaping wolf's soft flank. Loosing his jaws to howl in pain, the brute fell sprawling in the snow.

Without a sound the two young wolves were at his throat, tearing out his life, while up above, the cradle-board hung for the moment safe. And in a ring about the struggling three, the pack drew in to watch—with wicked slanting eyes and open jaws a-grin—the outcome of the fight.

In tumbling, squirming, snarling mass the wolves rolled to a little distance. Then a straggler perceived that swaying thing above. The little warm and pulsing life called out with fierce temptation to the killer beast. He leaped, caught hold and pulled the child to ground.

Once more Kioga brought the whip lash into play—one stinging cut to draw the wolf's attention to the raw red slash it made. Before the echo of the stroke had blown away, Kioga jumped.

Full twenty feet he dropped in breathless fall, crushed the wolf down deep into the snow, slung the cradle-board upon his back, and like a flash leaped upward, grasping the limb from which the child had dangled.

His speed had served him well, but only by the thickness of a skin—the skin of which his furry garb was made. For as he drew himself aloft, long rows of gleaming teeth snapped viciously, hooking off a strip of skin and laying bare his leg. Six wolves fought hotly to possess the leather, and shredded it to ribbons.

From above, Kioga loosed the vials of his wrath upon them: "O Gobblers-of-Ancient-Bones! O Slayers-of-the-Helpless! Blunted be thy fangs, and may thy whelps be born with eyes that cross! O Cowards-of-the-Forest, may skunks invade thy dens, and at the end the meat-birds peck thy yellow eyes out!" And as he spoke, Kioga plied the lash with cunning malice, stinging one wolf, that it might think another had ripped it from behind, until two separate brawls progressed below.

Kioga's bared leg grew cold; to get back to the cave was imperative. And now the little swaddled creature slung upon his back gave out a hunger-cry.

The distance from the solitary tree to the ravine ledge Kioga measured with his eye. Another time he would have chanced a leap, success a probability. But with this cradle-board upon his back, two lives would be the cost of one least slip upon the icy footing. Nor dared he linger here for fear of freezing to death.

Along the edge of the ravine he glimpsed a stout protruding root. Upon this root he flicked the loose end of his whip and saw it lap three times around. Testing it, he felt it bind securely. Below, the wolves were still at grips among themselves when taking hold upon the handle of his whip, Kioga dropped through space. One short breath-taking instant he swung down, not more than inches high above their heads. Before the pack took notice, Kioga clung safely to the sheer side of the ravine, beyond the point at which the whip was fixed.

Loosening and drawing in the coil, Kioga

climbed still higher to the top of the ravine. Then through the eddying swirls of snow he hastened back toward the cave where Mika slept.

Along the route he paused to kick the snow from the spike-buck's carcass; and from the kill, now frozen stiff, he broke off a ham. New paw-marks at the cave-mouth showed that Mika had prowled out recently. Within the cave, of leaves and twigs Kioga made a little fire, started with thong and drill from his belt-pouch. Outside the den he found firewood and brought it in.

Against the wall he set the cradle-board and put the haunch of venison to thaw, returning next to contemplate the stoic little bright-eyed mote of life that he had snatched from the grim powers of the wilderness.

Designs upon the cradle-board denoted a child from the tribe known as the People-of-the-Plume, the Wacipi, foremost musicians of all the Shoni nation. Then in the growing light he saw another mark, a small blue circle on that smooth brown brow, the sign of lofty rank among the Wacipi.

"Son of a higher chief!" Kioga breathed in surprise. "What do you out in such a storm? The walls of Magua are high and strong. The gates are closed when such as you would venture forth. *Ehi*—this has the smell of wickedness! But that can wait. Here, eat." And Kioga held a chunk of hot and dripping meat to his foundling's lips.

Wild children early learn to crave the taste of flesh. The two-year-old ate much and rapidly. And as it ate, Kioga pondered aloud:

"All winter long, I alone of Hopeka-town go forth into the snows when there is not the need. How is it then, that a woman of Magua comes roaming out, a child upon her back, alone? It smells of wickedness, I say—how or why, I do not know. But never mind, my little chief, I'll take thee back, to the very walls of Magua, and there we'll learn—"

Kioga did not finish, for as he spoke, a plume of steam blew in at the entrance to the cave. Two round and steady flames came in, behind them the sinuous length of Mika, snow upon his fur. Glimpsing the child, the puma crouched and bared white fangs and snarled. When Mika sought to pass, Kioga cuffed the animal roughly as only he would dare. In the end the puma retreated to a corner.

All unaware, the infant fell asleep. Once more the only sounds were the soughing of the winds beyond the cave, the rustle of embers settling in the fire, or the crackle when Kioga threw on a handful of fresh twigs and wood. Now and then Mika made a stealthy move to circle round Kioga, but settled back each time the boy's gaze fixed him.

Time passed. The sharp report of bursting trunks bespoke a sudden drop in temperature out in the forest.

The pile of twigs was nearly gone. Kioga hacked some pieces from the cradle-board and finally removed the child completely, slinging it upon his back by the leather thongs, then burned the entire board. This was his last resource. The wood was gone, and he dared not trust Mika with the child while he sought more outside.

And then the fire gutted out. The cave was almost dark—save for the embers' ruddy glow. The panther crept a little nearer—Kioga heard the ominous scratch of claws.

Then suddenly there came diversion from without—a heavy thunderous growl, but muffled by passage through banked-up snow. Then came the tear of hooks through snow and ice. The armor which had locked them in the cave crashed through like isinglass, admitting gusts of stinging snow and fresh air.

A mighty paw, broader than three men's hands laid side by side, intruded, studded thick with long curved claws all blunted at the ends. A bear's vast head appeared, haloed by the sickly glimmer of the northern lights.

The eyes were small, close-set, a wicked red. The open-hanging jaw uncovered black and stumpy teeth, the canines worn and split with age. A roar burst from the twitching lips, and Mika answered with a fierce and warning scream, his earlier threat to the child forgotten before this common danger—an aged solitary bear come home to claim its winter den.

Its burly shoulders filled the entrance. Three living lesser things pressed back against the inner wall. Upon the red-hot embers the bruin dropped a paw and roared anew with doubled fury, then with a lumbering rush charged through on the intruders.

In desperate defense Mika drove curving sickles deep and fastened fiercely on the bear's head and shoulders. Back and forth between the cramping narrow walls the battle raged and roared, with Mika slowly being worsted.

Then, quick as thought, Kioga saw his chance—the bear's left paw up-reached to claw the puma to the ground. As snake's tongue darts, Kioga's knife licked swiftly forth, and back, and forth again—

three deep and telling thrusts that found the bear's aorta. The brute reared up, then crumpled on its quarters, and rolling over, fought no more.

The way to liberty was clear. Without delay Kioga took his opportunity, the infant on his back. Mika remained behind to make a long and satisfying meal.

At large again, out where the air was clean and pure, Kioga saw the storm-racked heavens clearing of their clouds. The winds were silent; and on silent feet Kioga turned toward the ravine.

The wolves had gone upon another chase. Among the little they had left of what had been a woman, Kioga picked up some copper ornaments, a head-band, a string of beads and other little trinkets. Then he turned toward Magua, the village of the child which was slung on his back.

Few forest prowlers were abroad. Without mishap these wanderers of the midnight, hurrying along the frozen rivers, drew nearer to the northern village. And in proportion as they neared, Kioga watched ahead more carefully for signs of hunters or those wayfaring in the wilderness. Ahead, against the trees, he caught a golden glow thrown by a camping-fire. Another might have gone ahead boldly; but Kioga, lone hawk of the wilderness, approached with all the stealth of a lynx. Friends or foes he wished to see, before being seen.

From beneath a branch that cast a solid shadow he looked forth upon a band of scouts squatting round about their fire, with painted robes drawn close about their shoulders. Lean stalwart redskinned men they were, without warpaint, but wearing each his weapons in sheath and quiver. A little nearer Kioga drew to hear their words.

" 'Tis passing strange," said one as if in answer to an earlier question. "*Iho!* More than strange, that the child should vanish from our very midst."

"Think you so?" queried another, less doubtfully. "The like has been before, Catesa."

"Ah, when the shamans took a child for sacrifice, indeed. But this is otherwise—the mother vanished too. Wayona was a favored wife of Twenty Scalps. Her issue would inherit chieftainship."

"So, so?" said the other warrior in surprise. "Then there is mystery here. Some one had cause to put this only child away. Some one,"—with a shrewd glance about the circle,—"who would gain by such an act."

Catesa raised his brows a little. "You mean—Otakte of the crooked hand?"

The other spread his hands before the blaze. "I do not mean a thing," he answered warily. "But anyone can guess."

"There would be great reward for him who brought Wayona and her child back home again," interposed a third warrior thoughtfully.

"All Magua would be too small to honor such a one!" agreed Catesa.

Kioga listened carefully. About to give the child up to these friendly warriors with the story of all that had befallen, he checked himself. Here was the chance to gain that for which any boy yearns— honors, recognition by the tribal elders. Here would be requital for his outcast days!

In Magua, a village not his own, he would be honored, made much of, his bravery lauded to the winter skies. Already he had visions of how the news would spread, and how Hopeka-town would at last put on gala dress when he returned triumphant. With that alluring thought, he changed his mind. With growing pride he swelled his chest, then left the winter camp behind and journeyed on toward Magua.

The fires of the northern river-village threw a glow against the white-sheathed forest overhanging its walls.

"Now," said Kioga, to that silent sleeping mite upon his back, "I'll take thee in. But not through open doors. Eh, no! Things that are good are often best done quietly. We'll enter by another way—I've done the same before, last summer with the trading men. I know a certain log that offers hold for hand and foot."

Without a sound Kioga scaled the wall, dropping with his little burden inside the village of Magua. A lodge near by reflected firelight. Stealing to its side, Kioga ascertained that no one was within. Here, to be lighter for his venture through the populous village, he laid the child and left it, still sleeping.

"Wayona will suckle thee no more. Some one has done a mighty wrong. A punishment is due. When that is done, I'll hope for something better than words of thanks. Now I will seek Otakte of the crooked hand. If I recall aright, he tends the sacred fire that burns in the medicine-lodge."

Kioga walked boldly forth into the village proper. The sounds of rhythmic music amplified as he drew near the dancing-ground. The deep low chants of men came in a stirring chorus. An ancient day of holiness was being celebrated. Among the increasing throng Kioga passed easily as a youth of Magua.

But near the entrance to the medicine-lodge he

shed his boldness, glanced up and down, then stepped into its purple shadow. Beside the door he paused a moment, listening with his owl-keen ears to learn if anyone was within. Then melting through the hanging skins, he stood alone inside the walls.

This was a strange and crowded place, filled up with ceremonial objects. Masks and shields hung along the wall. Rich robes were draped from racks, row after row, one close upon another. At the height of a tall man above, rough-hewn shelves contained a hundred different garments for the dance or feast.

At one end of the lodge a little fire burned perpetually, in a hole dug in the ground. From this, each year, the village fires were kindled afresh. Otakte must soon return to see that the sacred fire still burned. Failing in this, his lifelong trust, the penalty was death. . . .

Otakte came back sooner than the Snow Hawk had expected, and more quietly. A rustle at the door was Kioga's first warning. Without a sound he drew behind the robes that curtained off one side of the lodge, then from concealment observed Otakte narrowly.

Otakte was in genial mood. He rubbed his hands and warmed them at the fire; he chuckled often and contentedly; he lit and smoked his pipe, and blew smoke rings above his head. Once he laughed aloud in great good humor with himself, then rose and strutted back and forth before the fire. And presently another joined him.

The door-skin rose, admitting a village warlock, old and stooped, and formed like a djinni from a fairy tale. He strode in triumphantly, barefooted for all the cold, and clad in a tattered blanket he always affected as evidence of humility.

"Welcome, Man-of-Magic," sounded Otakte's greeting. "Draw near beside the sacred fire, and warm thy holy bones, and smoke a pipe with me."

"*Eh-hee!* Right gladly that I will," the other lisped through toothless gums. "Methinks we have more cause to celebrate than they!"—holding up a hand to indicate the music from the village.

"Indeed, Okeela, you are a shrewd one," said Otakte admiringly. " 'Twas you who found the way to make my son become a ruling chief."

Okeela spread his warty hands and gave a modest laugh. " 'Tis nothing."

" 'Tis everything," Otakte contradicted him; "and cheaply won."

"*Ai,* now that is true," Okeela laughed. "We have not even taken life to gain our ends. Eh, true enough—Wayona took her babe and went into the forest when I told her that its name was on the shaman's lips for sacrifice. And then a storm came up and she has not returned. Whose fault is that? Not ours, indeed. The forest gods favor our acts. This is the proof."

But there was one, himself no small influence in the forest, who heard without approval. Kioga's brows drew together in a scowl. Ambition—here he saw it at its worst—ambition of the kind which crows about ignoble ends, won by deceit at little risk. "The smell of wickedness grows ever stronger. What more?" he wondered silently. Almost as if in answer, Otakte spoke.

"What if Wayona should escape the storm and return?"

"Then it will be time to use the knife," replied

Okeela harshly, and added more which Kioga did not hear, for he had slipped to the entrance, softly raised the skin and left the lodge.

Back to where he had left the child he went, and took it on his back again, and at a trot ran toward the house of Twenty Scalps. The distance was not great from one wall to another; but as the Snow Hawk swung round a corner, he saw a group of people congregated, and coming toward him a bent and crooked figure—Okeela.

Kioga checked—Okeela, too, his black quick eyes instantly noting the child upon Kioga's back. Okeela knew—it was his business to—that Kioga was not a youth of Magua. Almost at once he recognized Kioga's burden for the son of Twenty Scalps, and with the knowledge gasped in sheer astonishment.

But he was sharp and cunning. Okeela raised a bony forefinger and pointed at the Snow Hawk.

"*Aya-yalai!* Who are you, boy? Where go you with that child?"

"Back to the lodge of Twenty Scalps," Kioga answered, essaying to push his way beyond the shaman. Okeela seized him by the arm, and with a shrill yell drew forty pairs of eyes upon them.

"*Hai,* worthy folk of Magua! Behold the stealer of a high-born child! Fall on him! Out with his eyes!"

"A moment!" said the commanding voice of a chief among the throng. A tall and stately figure stood forth from the press and took the child up in his arms, inspecting it intently. "In truth, this is the child of Twenty Scalps." And turning to Kioga, "How came you by him, boy?"

"I saved him from the wolves," Kioga cried

loudly that all might hear. "The pack has killed his mother."

"A likely tale," shrieked the shaman, beside himself with rage and guilty fear at this failure of his schemes. "He stole him from the mother, whom he slew. Behold the blood upon his furs."

"'Tis not the truth," Kioga shouted stoutly. "Bear's blood this is, upon my furs—blood of the bear I slew to save our lives."

"The bear he slew—*ha-ha!*" mocked Okeela in derision. "Defies T'yone and his pack! Destroys a bear—'tis nothing! What next is there for him to lie about?" And with the words, Okeela snatched at Kioga's belt-pouch.

The ornaments Kioga had taken from the victim of the wolves fell out upon the ground. Okeela yelled in triumph, turning to the populace, gathering now from everywhere. "Behold—the rings and strings and bracelets of Wayona, favored wife of Twenty Scalps. How now,"—to Kioga, with a deadly sneer,—"were these Wayona's gift, my honest youth?"

"Not so," Kioga answered, visions of great honors dwindling. "I took them from among her bones."

"He took them from among her bones!" derided Okeela, with a high shrill laugh, the cackle of the rabble-rouser. "Was ever falser tongue than this? He stole them! Why do we wait? Away with him! The tribal penalty for stealing a Wacipi child! Tie him up outside the wall along a tiger's beat—then let him tell the truth!"

Still the multitude did not respond, until Otakte of the crooked hand, arriving on the scene to see his hopes for his own son crumbling, beheld the danger to dreams of power, and rushed upon Kioga. Another savage followed suit, another still. Then all the senseless mob, its herding instincts fanned by the shaman's words, closed in upon Kioga.

In vain he shouted out above the din what he had heard within the medicine-lodge. His voice was as a breath drawn in a hurricane. A score of hands tore at him, and held him out at painful stretch. Out through the gate they bore him, struggling.

But as they went, Kioga suddenly ceased to squirm, for something still unknown to the mob from Magua came to Kioga through the medium of his sharper nostrils.

Without a word he let them tie him up against a sapling thickly sheathed in ice, in view to all of Magua's populace. With stoic face he endured it when Okeela spat upon him; nor did he flinch when others threatened him with their knives, played round about his head. But when they turned to go, Kioga made a last demand.

"A bow, a full quiver—a bit of meat—the right of all who are to die," he said without emotion. One of the warriors, obedient to the ancient custom, paused to leave these things beside the doomed boy. Then all departed; and ranging behind the walls of Magua, prepared to watch the drama on the hill-top, when Guna of the hundred stripes should come along and find a captive tethered ready for his fangs.

Still in his bonds, Kioga did not struggle, but with the patience of the Indian he was by training, waited for what his nose had told him soon would happen—the coming of the bears of Indegara. Down-wind they were, and so he could not scent them at the moment. But call he did, a shrill and penetrating whistle that echoed from the village walls, and sounded for a mile into the still white wilderness. One note he sounded, then waited.

But what he heard was not the sound he wanted. A tiger's jarring note shook white flakes from the branches just above. Upon the breeze a dread scent came; and looking to the north, Kioga saw a grayish form stride into view.

Guna was coming on the prowl, his great paws loosely swinging, massive head close to the ground, long belly-hair brushing the snow, his furry tail up-curled. Regally he slouched along, careless as befits the emperor-king of all the killer-cats that walk the earth.

A mighty shout betrayed excitement running high behind the walls of Magua. And with the sound the tiger glimpsed the prey and crouched to stalk Kioga. More slowly now, the muscles rolled beneath that perfect coat. Flat on the snow the active tail now quivered, twitching only at its end.

Then suddenly the hue and cry in Magua died down, replaced by a hush of silent wonderment. What the villagers saw from a distance, Kioga saw close by.

The tiger crouched to spring upon him, rose up with arching back instead, retreating step by step with wet fangs bared, and snarling in his fury.

Down the trail, advancing in a slow and ominous swagger, a huge she-bear came lumbering. On either side of her, a little back, a half-grown bear-cub shuffled. Then from behind, four other shaggy heads came into view, and after them many more.

Along the palisade a warrior spoke, in tones of awe: "The gathering of the bears! Look! See their numbers! Even Guna of the hundred stripes retreats!"

He spoke the truth. The tiger disappeared. The bears were milling round the tree to which Kioga was bound. Some reared erect to gaze straight toward Magua. Amid their throng Kioga could not be seen.

But licking at his cold and tethered hands, the quick hot tongue of his old friend small Aki had already done what no amount of straining could have achieved—melted some of the ice upon the knots, thus loosening the leather cords a little. Kioga, conscious of the easing tension, writhed and strained within the cords. . . . A little later he was free, and threading his way among the bearpeople to an eminence whence he could command a view of Magua. A shout rose up:

"He is free! . . . He goes unharmed among the forest people!"

Along the wall two figures stood apart from the village throng. Of these, one was Okeela, the other Otakte, tender of the village fire, bow in hand and arrow on the string.

"Unharmed—but not for long!" he muttered, sighting down the shaft and letting fly at little more than point-blank range. But what with his haste, the whistling arrow flew aside and pierced one of Kioga's bears.

With lightning fingers Kioga whipped forth an arrow of his own and sent it singing at Otakte. The Snow Hawk's shaft flew true. Otakte saw it coming. To save himself, he jerked Okeela before him. Pierced through the breast, the shaman wheeled, reached for his knife, and in retaliation sought to lay Otakte low, but age and his wound deprived him of the power.

But as he fell, he called the name of Twenty Scalps, and in a dying voice confessed their double guilt in the matter of Wayona's death.

Eyes blazing, Twenty Scalps turned upon Otakte, his tomahawk uplifted; but Otakte took a defiant stance.

"You dare not strike. I am the keeper of the sacred fire. I am immune to punishment."

Twenty Scalps drew back, the blow unstruck, his eyes aflame with boundless hatred. But then another voice was heard, a woman's cry, ringing with religious hysteria through all Magua:

"The sacred fire has just gone out! Ten years of hardship threaten us—unless Otakte dies."

Otakte, pale, dismayed, turned to run. But with one sudden mighty blow, Twenty Scalps clove him to the eyes.

In all the rush of these events Kioga and his bears had been forgotten. When again the folk of Magua looked forth, the snowy hillside was alive with giant shadows, disappearing two by two around a ridge. Upon the back of one, Kioga rode astride, their shadows black against a shieldlike moon.

As he vanished, one warrior said to another in Magua: "Unless I had seen, I would not now believe this thing."

The other pondered thoughtfully, then answered: "I thought I recognized that face. He was Kioga—of Hopeka-town. What you have seen is nothing. He saved but one life here. Once the entire village of Hopeka was endangered. Ten times a hundred of the Shoni folk might then have died. I know, for I was there. Listen, and I will tell you of it."

But that's another tale.

PART IV

Flight of the Forest People

The seven Kindred Shoni Tribes are of a race who love the earth. They are a copper-skinned people, surviving wild cousins of the tamed American red man, who dwell beyond the shoulders of the earth, within the Arctic Circle, in a volcano-warmed land which they call Nato'wa. It has been known to man whose skins are white only within this present decade.

The Shoni tribesmen have good cause to revere their wilderness land, warmed by a mellow ocean current and by the inner fires of the earth, and thronged with game. But even more, perhaps, do they revere the forest rivers which link their savage kingdom together, and form their avenues of inter-tribal trade—and ofttimes of bloody war.

Each river has its patron god—so think the Shoni—and every cave and lake and shadowed glade its spirit of good or evil. Unto these spirits and gods the Shoni tribes make endless sacrifice. Sometimes this sacrifice is in the form of food, tossed on the waters, sometimes of ornaments hung on some sacred rock; again a man may make a sacrifice of weaponry, or cast his valued shield into a waterfall. More rarely the shamans give a human life, though happily this does not often occur. . . .

On the banks of the Hiwasi, two arrows' flight from old Hopeka-town, there is an image of a human head, carved in the rugged granite high on the cliffs through which the river flows.

The head upon the rock is handsome—a skilled, true likeness of a youth of fifteen, carved by the primitive sculptor Okantepek, whom all the mighty chieftains of the Shoni tribes engage to perpetuate their faces for the coming ages.

Okantepek would say, if asked about that youth's head carved in stone, "That is Kioga of Hopeka-town. He did a brave deed."

When springtime comes among the Shoni tribesmen, and the sinews of the river bulge and with a mighty effort break the icy chains of winter and course their channels once again, the tale is heard when the hunters gather about the watchfires. And if Guna of the hundred stripes halts in his prowling to chill the forest with his roar, or if T'yone of the wolfish clan sends up his hunger-howl, so much the fitter. For then the red men nod their heads and say: " 'Tis true: for hark—the forest folk speak their agreement. They too were there."

Okantepek, of Magua, a northern river village, tells the story best, for he was present. And when Okantepek recounts it, others listen to his tale, clapping hands to mouths in wonder. . . .

Spring came early to mysterious Nato'wa, the year when these events transpired. The sun, long absent on his winter journey from the Arctic, sent up red fanlike banners to herald his coming in the southern sky. The earthly heat, volcanic in its nature, which warms this newfound land, seemed aided in this office by unseasonably warm winds from out the south. The migrant birds from far away came north early that year, to roost in countless myriads amid the deep primeval forests of Nato'-wa, and fill the breezes with their homing calls.

Between two mighty mountains, and high above the forest stretching cloaklike down the valley, one lake especially was high abrim with water: Metinga, which means "a piece of sky" in the Shoni tongue, is so named for its summer turquoise color; it is a vast, deep basin, an old volcano crater; into it from gleaming glaciers far above the timber-line immense volumes of water yearly flow and are collected, and overflow in two great cataracts to form the white headwaters of the river Makalu, which drains into the Hiwasi.

Above the shining surface of Metinga, leaned outward as if admiring themselves in its mirror surface, two overhanging forest trees threw shadows down upon the water. Above, upon one of their limbs, a brilliant Nato'wan jay preened one wing and presently discovered his moving image just below, whereat he puffed out his breast and stared complacently.

As the jay stared, his wise eye sharpened. For on the liquid mirror just below, there suddenly appeared another face that looked straight upward into his. A handsome face it was, framed in an unruly tangle of blue-black hair, with brilliant greenish eyes whose light of quick intelligence gleamed forth from the well-browned face. Naked, well-muscled shoulders next rose up, and round the neck the jay saw a string of eagle-claws.

But suddenly another face appeared beside the boy's. This was no human face, but of the ursine clan—a mighty bear whose shadow dwarfed that of his human companion. As if agrin at some huge joke, the bear's jaws hung open, red tongue lolling, lips back-drawn, exposing shining teeth from ear to ear, the fear and dread of every other forest dweller. Unlike the youth, who was the soul of silence, the bear rose up with no pretense of caution, and dislodged a great stone that plunged, shivering the images upon the lake with a sudden splash.

A beat of wings, a shriek of shrill surprise, and Wi-jak was away. But not too far, for Wi-jak's curiosity is fully equal to his caution. Upon a limb above, the bright bird perched, uttering things that should not be repeated.

Some days before, when Kioga quit the village of Hopeka, quick-eyed Wi-jak had seen him go. When Kioga lurked in ambush and drove his arrow through a buck, Wi-jak was there to steal a meal. When the Snow Hawk met with Aki, Wi-jak it was who spread broadcast the news. Then he had lost their trail and spent the night upon that branch above the swollen lake, only to see Kioga rising, as it seemed, from its deep blue waters in the morning. And so the forest pirate cursed the boy again, for cursing is the specialty of Wi-jak and his kind.

Between two quick short laughs Kioga answered: "Be still, Wi-jak, O Waker-of-the-Dead! How can we hear the sounds of spring when you are shouting? Be still, *ehi!* Or I will spit thee upon an arrow, as sure as my name is Kioga!"

At sound of human voice Wi-jak grew silent, and other sounds were heard. From everywhere the music of running waters bubbled. An icy brooklet giggled somewhere underneath the rocks. A loon laughed out uproariously out on the still deep lake, and disappeared beneath the water. But Wi-jak listened as Kioga spoke again indignantly.

"Thou art a selfish tuft of feathers. We came here first and slept beneath this thicket—I and Aki. We are at peace with thee and thine, Wi-jak. Now off with you—be gone! My ears still ring!"

But Wi-jak only answered with a string of fiery forest oaths, albeit in a lesser voice. Even had he understood the boy's command to go, Wi-jak would still have lingered; for often in the recent past he had hovered near this strange youth who consorted with the forest brutes, and spied upon his strange adventures, and found them fascinating.

Pretending not to hear Wi-jak's warm compliments, Kioga addressed his monologue to his shaggy friend.

" 'Tis spring, Aki. Hear how the waters sing around us! The lake is overflowing, and all the streams are white with foam and spray."

Kioga threw a glance aloft to where a glacier capped a peak with silver; and as he watched, a blue-white piece of ice broke off and burst bomb-like on a rocky slope, showering down a glassy dust.

"An early season, this," Kioga went on. "But in Hopeka-town they'll welcome it with songs and feasts and dancing. And to Hopeka we shall go, O

Clumsy-foot, first down the mountain to the river Makalu, where I have hid a raft, on which we'll ride round all the bends to where the river pours into the Hiwasi. From there it is an easy trip. Mayhap along the way we'll lose the one above, who troubles us."

Squatted on his haunches, Aki of the mighty jaws attended as if he understood. Thus it was—because Wi-jak annoyed their waking hours—that Aki and the Snow Hawk turned valleyward again and left the swollen Lake Metinga far behind them. And but for the harsh persecutions of Wi-jak, vast tragedy had surely fallen on the Shoni nation. . . .

Down through the forest tangle Kioga and his bear companion made their way. Great Aki, sure of foot but vast of bulk, must often go the longer route. Kioga, more agile than the quickest acrobat, descended like a plummet from cliff to tall tree's top, and down the yielding branches at their supple ends, transferred from one upon another, falling like a gibbon, and with as little effort. When far ahead he waited a little while for Aki, and waiting, listened to the boisterous laughter of the running streams, all eager for their yearly springtime union with the mighty rivers.

All forest life was now astir. Birds whistled in the branches. Across the valley two elks were bugling back and forth. Somewhere a tree fell, cut through by Flint-tooth the beaver, making annual repairs to his home and engineering works. Aki then came swinging into view, roaring with sheer gusto and joy of the season.

With Aki, then, as was his frequent habit, Kioga climbed to a ledge that overlooked his wilderness to have a look around. Emerging on the watching-place,—a cliff beside a waterfall that overlooked the forest round about,—he suddenly felt a subtle change, the first foreshadowing of trouble. The birds were still; the wapiti no longer bugled.

Then he saw death. A crushed and broken fawn rode limply over the brink and dashed to pieces on the rocks so far below he scare could hear its fall.

And now it seemed to him the streams had changed their voices. They muttered, as with a threat. He saw for the first time that many were no longer pure and sparkling, but turbid with black earth and yellow silt.

Kioga and Aki walked a little way upstream. They saw a pocket of leaves and floating twigs become a lesser jam of branches. Then downstream came a stumpy log which burst the jam. A flying piece caught Kioga underneath the eye. The river seemed to growl at him. Instinctively he moved a little nearer Aki, and put one hand upon that mighty shaggy shoulder, speaking in a whisper.

"There's trouble brewing, Aki. I feel it in my bones. Hark you—no bird's note can be heard. How still the forest it! And yet the waters talk more loudly than ever I have heard them before."

Great Aki whined, deep in his chest and shook his shaggy head uneasily. Kioga pointed upward. "Behold, the Birds of Death are circling and holding council in the air above Metinga. They know that something evil soon will happen. They always come beforehand. I hate them, Aki! Come, let us see what's brewing. But first—a drink." Suiting the action to the words, Kioga bent down beside a flowing spring to cup the liquid to his lips. But as at the waving of a magic wand, the water disappeared. A little moistened sand was all his hand scooped up. The font went dry before their eyes.

"Eh-hu!" Kioga muttered, "The earth begrudges us a drink. And hark! I hear the sound of rumbling. . . . Come, Aki!"

Back up the slope they went, not pausing until they stood again where earlier Wi-jak had broken in upon their slumbers. One single glance Kioga flung across the lake, then caught his breath. For here and there upon the surface, great oily bubbles rose, and bursting, gave forth a strange unpleasant stench. And even as they watched, there was a tremor of the earth. A great crack formed along the solid rocky wall which held the impounded waters of Metinga in a kind of natural dam. There was the fearful sound of tree-roots parting like pack-thread well below the surface of the earth, and thunder shook the ground beneath their feet.

Had a tiger sprung upon him, Kioga would have leaped away, and probably escaped. But when the very earth convulses, it is the better part of common sense to wait, stock-still. Tense, yet cool as ice, Kioga waited for what might come, as oftentimes before, when quakes disturbed his forests. Beside him, the usually fearless Aki quivered.

There was a stillness, fraught with apprehension. Then with a hissing sound, a geyser rose within the lake—a gigantic mushroom of water. When it fell, drenching them with chilly spray, two cylindrical rods of water under fearful pressure burst from the south wall of Metinga, and shot forth horizontally, shearing off stout trees like candle-wax.

And then, from far above, there came the roar of avalanche. Cracked by the tremors of the earth and loosened by the warmth of early spring, the half of one great glacier was tumbling down the mountain, immensely adding to the weight of old Metinga's stored-up waters. Beneath that added pressure the southern wall gave way. Not all at once, or Kioga and Aki had been engulfed, but slowly at the first, and with the fearful groan of rock on rock.

As with one mind Aki and Kioga turned tail and sought a higher level still, wherefrom they watched with staring eyes the dying of an age-old lake. The pressure of the water told. Great streams, each a cataract in size, burst from the crumbling rock. Then with the crash of field-artillery, the whole shell of the ancient crater bulged and leaped outward. Havoc, terror and destruction rushed upon the valley in the path of Metinga's flood.

A wall of water eighty feet in height and many more across, a mighty river roaring where a creek had babbled, its rushing crest already a chaos of uprooted trees and forest trash—that was what Kioga and Aki looked upon from fancied safety on a slope above the foaming flood; but even there they were not immune to the giant's clutch of the monster just unleashed.

Hardly had the first crest swept past, when the forest slope on which they stood began to slip, undermined by the racing tide. A quarter-mile of virgin timber took leave of its rocky moorings and coasted toward the flood.

Kioga and the bear, entrapped among the tottering trees, rode downward with the ragged square of forest; and with them went uncounted other living creatures who chanced to occupy the area before it slipped away. Until it reached the flood, the land-slip held together, while on its sliding surface the hunter-killers ceased pursuit, and the hunted ones stood rooted and sought no longer to escape.

A weary buck at bay beheld the wolf-pack falter as the ground beneath them heaved and groaned. A tiger, poised to launch his killing rush, saw prey and forest roar away to leave the rocky bones of earth laid bare. Then with a rush the land-slip plunged into the waters. Great forest giants tossed about like twigs, and in their ponderous convulsions bludgeoned all that came into their path.

For others they were floating haven. Locked by fangs and claws to such a great tree, mighty Aki clung with all his strength. And onto Aki, Kioga clung with grim tenacity, dodging tossing limbs and tangled roots. Their tree turned over, dragging both beneath the surface, then righted, raising them aloft again. Then plunging like a monstrous brute, berserk among a thousand tossing others of its kind, their tree rushed wildly forward on the swirling waters. Kioga and Aki were a part of chaos, and not the only ones engulfed.

A luckless half-drowned tigress struggled to draw herself upon the log, but could not summon strength. Into her fear-filled eyes the Snow Hawk gazed. Although in other circumstances Gunahi would have eaten him with relish, now they shared a common danger. Mutual peril raised a truce. Pity filled Kioga while she struggled, slipping slowly back. Laying hold upon her heavy tail he sought to drag Gunahi from the water, while

Aki watched and showed his teeth, and roared in harsh hostility.

But when Kioga shouted at him, Aki, with many a distasteful grunt, took grip upon the tigress' heavy ruff. And so, between them both, they hauled her onto their log—a sorry-looking forest baroness, too spent to more than bare her fangs and twitch her wet, bedraggled tail.

Now from the other side a stag swam alongside, with fear-distended eyes. By one antler Kioga seized him, and drew him trembling up to sanctuary.

From time to time other creatures, hard beset, sought safety on this only stable thing in all the boiling press about them. A mother-wolf came with her one surviving pup between her jaws, and was not turned away. A nest containing birds dangled from a limb sweeping past. The little downy things cried out, and at the risk of life and limb Kioga reached, seized, overbalanced, but recovered, saving all the nestlings. A troop of forest birds winged above to the plunging tree and settled on its upreaching boughs which once had been their home, all agitation, their young destroyed.

Thus laden with its birds and beasts, the strange ark raced on the tides of Metinga, with Kioga as its only human occupant. Sometimes it skirted close to shore, again yawed widely on the middle currents. All the Snow Hawk's efforts to guide it to the bank were as an ant's breath against a mainsail. But reach the bank he must, for into mind this thought had leaped, to strike fear for others into him who was fearless on his own account.

"Hopeka-town lies in the path of this onrushing flood!"

He had a momentary vision of the greatest Shoni village, filled with warriors and powerful chiefs from every distant clan and tribe along the river-ways. He visualized the dancers in their full regalia, the singers lifting up their voices in thanksgiving for this early spring—while down upon them rushed disaster. He saw beloved Mokuyi and Awena, his Indian foster-parents, caught upon the dread white bubbling crest and dashed into eternity. He saw Hopeka's walls and dwellings leveled, swept away, a blow from which the Shoni nation would not recover for a generation.

How long before this racing flood would overwhelm the Shoni capitol and sweep the canoe argosies into nothingness? Kioga knew the route the river Makalu described. He knew its many serpentine turns and twists, and where it emptied into the Hiwasi. And one thing more he knew—the one defile through which a man afoot might pass, and granting that he were swift, attain Hopeka in time to warn its celebrants.

A man afoot—upon that thought he looked about him at the havoc on the surface. Ahead the crest was well advanced, destroying as it went. Miles behind already Metinga Lake was still outspilling its vast quantities of water, adding to the tidal wave. And all around, a wilderness of trees tossed and pitched wildly. To seek to gain the shore across the jam was suicide.

He glanced ahead again. A bend showed in the river, and toward it their ark was rushing. The seething waters carved deep into the bank, and damming up, forced Kioga's tree away toward mid-river. Then suddenly a back-eddy seized its crown and swung it in toward shore, beneath the cut-under bank.

Kioga saw his chance and raced along the bole. Catlike, he sprang upon a limb, and leaping, caught a dangling slippery root, maintained his grip and clambered up. The wet root snapped. Kioga grasped another.

A moment more, and he was safe. He paused a second to look back. The log, still bearing up its many occupants, rushed onward. A lump was in Kioga's throat, and seeing was not easy through the mist that came before his vision at sight of faithful Aki, upreared upon the disappearing tree and calling in a mighty voice to one who never in the past had deserted.

Then, low of heart, the Snow Hawk turned away, taking comfort from the thought that Aki had a chance for life, at least. But who in all Hopeka-town would still survive if no one warned them of the coming torrent?

On flying feet that spurned the earth Kioga fled along a forest trail, worn smooth by countless hordes of brutes who wander through the forests of Nato'wa. Then from the trail he turned obliquely and up a mountain-side began to climb.

The rocks were slippery with melting snow, but no chamois had ever surer feet than he. Up and up Kioga went, taking hand-hold where he found it, seizing roots and spurs of rock to draw himself aloft. Sometimes his ascent was slow, but oftener he leaped and sprang with panther's ease and speed. For all that he made haste, scarce a stone did those light steps disturb in mounting to the summit.

Along the ridge he ran, hair blown straight out

behind him, a shadow black against a sunset sky.
Then through the rocky pass which cuts uncounted miles of travel from the forest roamings of the
Shoni scouts and messengers, and down into the
valley, Kioga raced with grim catastrophe, and
came toward the valley as if hell-hags were hard
upon his heels.

Here flowed the broad Hiwasi, whose distant
reaches lapped the bank at Hopeka. To a well-hid-
den place Kioga went, and poked around among
the thickets, uncovering at last a good light bark
canoe and paddle, cached there the season past
when early winter and a sudden freeze caught him
far from home.

He lifted the canoe and placed it on the water.
It leaked, but time did not permit repairs. Taking
up his paddle, Kioga drove it deep and sent the
craft gliding out into the middle currents.

The deep Hiwasi, too, was swollen, and all its
tributary streams were adding to its size. The
banks were inundated, the water-level risen
twenty feet. The yearly river-ravages were just begun, and for that the Shoni would be prepared.
But when that white-headed roaring flood, as yet
far up the winding valley of the Makalu, did
come, it must wreak a frightful havoc—unless Kioga came in time.

Ahead his quick eye sought a certain waterfall
he knew, which he must portage his canoe around.
As he drew near, the place appeared, not now a
drop of forty feet, but thanks to rising waters, a
lesser rushing current which fell but twenty in a
long low arc. A carry here would cost him precious
minutes in his race to bear a warning to Hopeka-
town. He scanned the white-capped waves beyond

the fall, for there the greatest danger lurked. Then he looked long and searchingly up the valley of the Makalu.

There was not time to make the carry even if he wished, for near enough for seeing with the naked eye, he glimpsed the birds of death, wheeling and funneling in the sky. That meant the racing crest moved swifter than he had anticipated. As it moved, it carried dead and dying creatures on its flood. And where death is, the forest scavengers are always near.

Now with a calculating eye upon the waters he gently urged his birch-bark forward. He knew the dire risks of these unyielding rips below. Not for nothing had Kioga ridden back and forth with the red-skinned traders from Hopeka-town. But with a cool and level gaze he faced it, risks and all.

He felt the swelling current seize the flimsy fabric of his craft. With cunning touch he dipped and held, or twisted on the handle of his blade to hold his bow upon a rock that showed up far below the point of peril. But though the river had borne him on its breast before, it now was definitely hostile, and on a deep and fearful note roared down between its banks. The very winds had changed and caught his bow and gave a twist that almost robbed him of control. A great rock, shifting on the changing river-bottom, upturned, and with its sharp edge skived deeply through the barken side of his canoe, and water entered. Kioga shifted balance slightly to bring the damaged part above the waterline.

He cut inshore, to skirt a whirlpool that seethed between two rocks; and hardly had he passed when down the crumbling perpendicular wall a hundred tons of granite toppled, hurling him forward on its mighty wave. Each time disaster skimmed him just a little closer.

The forest, hitherto impartial, had turned its other face. He felt forces, grim, malign, leaguing up against him. He thought of all the Shoni superstitions relating to the river-gods, and gripped his paddle a little tighter. For white-skin though he was by heredity, association with the Indians of the Shoni tribes had filled his head with curious halfbeliefs which now crept into mind with sinister suggestion.

"The forest gods have turned against me.... O Thing-of-Bark, be light and fleet! A thousand lives now ride betwixt thy slender ribs. For if Kioga comes too late, Hopeka is no more."

An Indian, thus apprehending danger from the many gods he feared, would have given up resistance, and let the waters bear him where they would. Not so with Kioga of the blue-green eyes and paler skin. In him there was a different spirit, daring to pit itself against the hostile powers of the wilderness, even in this, their angry mood.

An instant more, and he was on that bulging central current of the cataract. The bank fled past, the light craft racing like a thing alive. Then came a leap, a mighty surge. As if on wings the small canoe shot forth upon the brink, and there a moment poised. Kioga felt a sinking motion; then his craft slipped swiftly over the fall and down amid the stiff and curling waves of the rapids.

Crouching low with ready blade, he held his cockle-shell upon a steady course. All about, the snarling river gnashed, and sought some grip upon that smooth and fragile fabric, which by its very lightness bobbed along almost in safety. But with the greatest danger well behind, Kioga saw the straining seams give way. A vicious wave broke hard across the bow, and in an instant overturned the fleeing craft.

Kioga plunged before the canoe dipped under. Sport of the whirling currents, he struck out for the nearest bank. The waters whipped and spun him. He seized a floating log. An eddy swung him into quiet water. On the bank he rested panting, almost spent, but with the knowledge of his duty still before him. Then swiftly down the bank he fled, and heaved a sigh of deep relief when Hopeka's walls came into view.

Drawing near, the Snow Hawk heard the old men's voices rising in deep hosannas, and answering, the ringing chorus of the women's song. He heard the undertone of drums, the peal of sacred whistles, the silken rustle of the deer-hide rattles. He turned an instant toward whence he had come, and sought to translate the muttering of the waters into knowledge of when the crest would come. The river was swollen to within ten feet of the palisades.

He stood before the heavy gate and beat upon it fiercely with his fist. A sentry's head appeared; the gate swung in. Kioga entered, threw a glance about, and saw a hundred faces that he knew.

Sawamic, the Shoni emperor-chief, resplendent in his gleaming ceremonial robes; the circle of the shamans, squatted in the center of the dancing-place before the huge waist-high granite stone whereon the sacred village fire burned, from which each year the Shoni fires are rekindled; the long queue of the bending, leaping, naked dancers, winding in and out in mystic figures. . . .

All eyes were toward the stone, the center of attention; and all Hopeka listened raptly to the music, when suddenly, with catlike bound a supple figure sprang upon the fire-stone.

In loud and piercing tones Kioga raised his voice, pointing northward, up the river: "O Chiefs, and Elder Councilors, and people of Hopeka—rise up and flee! The waters of Metinga are soon upon you! Escape, before they come!"

The drums fell still. The sound of singing voices died away. Black as thunder grew the brows of the shamans at this fancied sacrilege. Slow Bull the warlock stood forth, fury in his eyes.

"Thou darest profane the sacred festival!" he cried. "O imp of mischief, I will punish thee!" And raising a tomahawk, Slow Bull advanced upon the Snow Hawk.

Then from his belt Kioga drew his long, well-sharpened knife and holding it poised for the throw, he faced the shaman grimly. "Another step, Slow Bull, and thou shalt feel my metal in thy heart!"

"You dare to threaten me?" cried Slow Bull in fury.

"I dare," replied Kioga, watching Slow Bull as a leopard would.

The shaman hesitated, liking not the steely gaze of that defiant figure on the fire-stone. And while he hesitated, Kioga addressed the others, speaking urgently:

"I come from far upriver. Metinga's wall has burst, and all its waters flood the valley of the Makalu. Make haste! An hour hence will be too late!"

"Ah, *bah!*" cried Slow Bull jeeringly. "What foolery is this! A youth gives orders to his chiefs, and flaunts the holy shamans to their very faces! Ho, warriors—fall upon the upstart!"

A rumble went among the great assembly, and from his rock Kioga saw that none believed him. From somewhere near, a stone was thrown, and caught the Snow Hawk on the shoulder, hurling him from the rock.

He sprawled before Slow Bull, who swung his tomahawk. Kioga dodged aside and the blow fell harmlessly. Slow Bull would then have made another stroke, when lean and sinewy fingers fell upon his wrist.

Kioga saw Mokuyi, his Indian foster-father, disarm the shaman. But as he ran, a dozen others would have seized him, for he had many mortal foes among the villagers. Eluding them, he turned toward the village gate and ran the gantlet, a shower of flying missiles clattering behind him.

He flung the great gate wide. And at what he saw upon the river Kioga checked, then swung round upon the spot and pointed, with a high, shrill yell: "Behold—all you who disbelieve!"

Two warriors came and looked with startled eyes upon the river's swollen width, then raised a cry which brought every person in Hopeka to the walls, to gaze in apprehension at a phenomenon.

From northward, down the river, the forest denizens of every clan came swimming. A troop of beaver, full two hundred strong, led the way, paddling swiftly past the village without a backward glance; and hard upon their heels uncounted mink and otter hastened. Behind them came bands of woodland caribou, their antlers clacking as they forged along white-eyed with fear.

Along the nearer bank a pack of wolves raced

southward, tails between their legs. When these had gone, three tigers passed, a mother with her two-year cubs. And panting almost on their heels an elk-stag, with his frightened harem, hurried by. Upon the distant shore a dozen mighty bears lumbered hastily; nor did they even pause to drink, despite their hanging, lathered tongues.

And then—something stranger still rushed past among the farther forest shadows, a thing of vaster bulk than any other brute. From Hopeka's wall the people looked, pointing, astounded at that uncouth shadowy shape for which they had no name. Of them all, but one had ever seen the monster brute before. Nor had Kioga name for what he saw. But what he sketched upon a bit of hide, which has endured, was unmistakably a living mammoth, surviving on no other part of earth except Nato'wa. . . .

Above the waters countless birds flew in a vast confusion and higher up, in swinging gyres, flew the purifiers of the forest—the giant buzzards and all their awful kin, the ravens and the carrion hawks. And even through the branches of the trees, innumerable squirrels and orange-breasted martens and other things which leap and climb, fled like a myriad silent shadows.

Then upon Hopeka there descended a horde of all the lesser creatures of the forest. Wood-rats and jumping mice, things that burrowed and things that crawled, with here and there among them their natural foes, the foxes and the weasel-tribe. Up all the palisaded walls they swarmed and overran the village, scurrying everywhere as if in search of haven, then fleeing on, a veritable tide of life intent on self-preservation, the first law of the wilderness.

And every brute among that legion, great and small, rode on the wings of fear. Some vast overwhelming instinct drove every one upon its headlong way.

Soon to the watchers on Hopeka's walls the apprehension grew infectious. A woman screamed:

"*Ai-ya—alai!* Take up what you own and flee! The forest gods are making war!"

The rush began and gathered swift momentum. All those who could, ran to their lodges, trampling those less agile as they ran. Mob-spirit ruled and all was wild upheaval, with only here and there a calm and stoic figure. Of these old Sawamic sought to raise his failing voice above the din and rally his warriors into orderly action, a losing effort as fear of death spread out like wildfire.

Upon the water-front there stood another, cool and quick to see the one way of escape. Small among the crowding, taller warriors, Kioga saw Mokuyi and Awena coming through the gateway, and to them passed an urgent message.

"Abandon the canoes. Take to the heights above the river-cliffs."

Without a word Mokuyi nodded and gathering others about him, began the climb. Then to the warriors Kioga shouted out his counsel. The great majority obeyed, but many more rushed helter-skelter to the great canoes lined up on the bank, and pushed off, putting their faith, as ever, in the water-way.

The exodus was now well under way. A little time would see Hopeka-town evacuated. But there were those less swift, who lagged behind, and through the gate Kioga rushed to lend them aid.

Metika, old and withered, he bore out in his arms and summoned two tall warriors to carry her aloft. Tokaya, with a broken leg in splints, he aided to the gate, where other hands took up his burden. Then he returned in search of any more in need of help.

Now from the heights there rose a sudden cry from many throats: "The waters of Metinga! The crest! The crest!"

Down in the condemned village Kioga heard that cry and rushed from lodge to lodge at speed redoubled. He found no one remaining and with a sense of duty well discharged, he sprinted to the gate and looked up-river.

A mile away he saw the yellow foaming crest approaching at a swift remorseless pace. He saw the several canoes, all laden deep with those who sought escape upon the river. He saw their paddlers cease their labors, and helpless, grasp the sides of their canoes, girding for the worst, their death-songs rising.

On roared the waters of Metinga, tearing mighty forests from their rootholds. The seething chaos loomed above the drifting war-canoes. Then like great chips the craft were snatched up and tossed, as from the horns of some gigantic bull, their human freight hurled every way. The solid craft rolled over and over, up-ended on the roaring crest, then were broken, crushed and pulverized between the milling trunks.

A moment, mesmerized by that evidence of primal power, Kioga watched death's drama, then turned to fly, when from the village came a cracked and broken voice, raising the death-chant of the Shoni people.

He knew it on the instant for the voice of Iska— Iska of the blinded eyes. And then he glimpsed her, as she groped along the village wall, a wizened, small, pathetic figure, the one forgotten soul in all of doomed Hopeka.

There stood one whose span of life was almost at its end. Upon her gazed Kioga, whose years were not a seventh of her own. From up above there came a distant warning: "Do not go back! The waters are upon you!"

Old Iska heard, and possibly divining, cried: "Escape! I'm old and worthless—I do not fear to die. Escape!"

"Escape, and leave thee here to die alone? Not I!" she heard, for answer. There came the padding sound of running feet. A quick hand took her own. The bellow of the waters mounted. But up above their roar came great shouts of encouragement from the cliffs, whence Hopeka's people saw a thrilling scene enacting.

Across Hopeka-town Kioga came, and through the open gate, then up the trail leading Iska by the hand, toward where a cheering populace watched, breathless, while the Snow Hawk matched his strength of will against the wild instinct to run from the threatening power of Metinga's oncoming waters.

Behind, the Snow Hawk heard the northern wall of Hopeka fall with a mighty splintering sound, and a quick glance back revealed the towering yellow-bubbled wave, then in the act of breaking full upon the village. An instant Hopeka stood forth, each detail clear in young Kioga's sight, the lodges, rambling streets, the fire-stone, its flame blown incandescent by the rush of air which had beaten down that northern wall.

Then as if some deathly spell were being cast, the site was whelmed in vast destruction. Hopeka-town was gone, all that it once had been now rushing toward the Caldrons of the Yei upon Metinga's tumultuous crest.

Once more Kioga turned to climb beyond the reach of danger. He sought to carry Iska. And then his strength, till now sustained by hurry and excitement, seemed draining from him. His feet were heavy. That slight weight of shriveled Iska, which at another time he would have borne with ease, was now too much. His breath came quick. His heart beat fast. Close behind the waters roared. Yet still he would not desert poor Iska, but turned to see the smothering foam rushing nearer. Within his naked breast Kioga's heart beat faster still, and yet with fearless eyes he faced his end without a tremor.

Valor begets its kind. Some one shouted from above:

"He falters. Aid him—quick!"

Three warriors formed a human chain, and at the risk of life and limb, lowered down within his reach. He put old Iska's wrists in the grasp of a clutching hand and stood back to watch her lifted to safety. But suddenly the other of that pair of hands seized hold on him. It was the iron grip of tall Okantepek—the One-Who-Cuts-the-Stone.

And thus, old Iska and Kioga were raised aloft.

Close beneath Kioga's dangling feet, Metinga's crest tossed up its foam, as from great jaws that snap and miss. Then in full roaring tide the flood churned along its boiling way, while eager hands hauled up Kioga and his human burden.

Now, while the people of Hopeka watched the passing of the waters, Kioga ate heartily of the meats and sweets with which the women plied him. But all the while his eyes were on the slowly falling river, eager for a glimpse of one he had abandoned far up-river, on the Makalu.

The waters fell yet lower, and still no sign of Aki, when suddenly Kioga bounded to his feet, a piercing whistle darting out across the river. Hopeka's homeless folk beheld a mighty fallen tree afloat upon the water. A tigress paced it restlessly. A wolf with cub crouched at one end beside a terror-stricken buck. Forward on the log a huge bear roared an answer to Kioga's whistle.

A flock of birds took wing as the great tree grounded with a jar. The buck sprang wildly ashore. The bear and other animals followed.

And then the villagers beheld a singular sight. A lithe brown youth sprang full upon the bear and on the bank they wrestled for a moment, then were gone. Hopeka's folk saw them later—high upon a pinnacle of stone, gazing after the receding fluid juggernaut that passed with muted thunder into distance. Then they were gone again, in search of other wilderness adventure.

The villagers filed down upon the clean-swept flat, all that remained of what was once Hopeka. When their early apathy had disappeared, they fell to work. A new Hopeka slowly rose upon the site.

But there was one who labored at a different kind of task. Okantepeg began cutting an image on a prominent cliff, at a point which marked the highest level to which the Hiwasi's waters had ever risen. . . .

One day, not long thereafter, Kioga chanced to pass. He saw the carven head, and knew it for his own. Beholding it, he laughed aloud. And as he laughed, a quick-winged jay alighted on a limb above his head, and cursed him in a loud and raucous voice. Kioga laughed again, this time without resentment of Wi-jak. Then to the great bear sitting at his side, he said:

"Okantepek carves skillfully. But there is something he forgot. I have the remedy for that."

Then from a belt-pouch he took a piece of flint, and standing on the ledge, scratched in, free-hand, a crude picture of a northern jay, above that other head. When he had done the Snow Hawk eyed his handiwork and cast a glance of merriment up at Wi-jak.

"It is your honest due, O Waker-of-the-Dead. For had you not awakened us to danger, Hopeka's folk had all been gone when we arrived."

The picture of Wi-jak has been eroded by the winds until a few faint scratches are all that now remain. The elements have had their way with Kioga's image, too.

But in the minds of Hopeka's red-skinned folk, the memory of those events is ever fresh. And if, in time to come, you chance to sit beside the watch-fires of the Shoni hunters, you'll hear the tale just as I have here unfolded it.

PART V

White Heritage

Below the forest of Indegara, where the great waves thunder in and smash to foam upon the southern coast of wild Nato'wa, there is a certain sheltered cove, above high-water mark.

Newfound Nato'wa is a cruel land. Dead things and their remains are plentiful amid its trackless wildernesses. But in that sheltered cove a dead thing lay which once had life and grace, and power to skim the seas like any gull. About her last remains the sad winds mourned. The hostile sea had struck her down and hurled her here to die. But never, since that storm-swept night, had the waters again risen up so far.

The broken bones of the little ship long bleached not far from where she struck. Vines grew up and down her sides; thorny underbrush hid the tarnished name-plate, which bore the one word *Cherokee*. Sometimes great white-toothed brutes sniffed about her broken decks; and on her tilted mast a colony of sea-birds had a favored perch.

For fifteen years the sad relics of the *Cherokee* had sunk slowly deeper into the concealing of the wilderness. In all that time no human glance or touch had fallen on her remains, when on a dark and shadowed rainy afternoon a vast primordial brute strode near on feet that scuffed the earth with careless laziness.

It was a bear—a creature like a grizzly, but on an even larger scale, as all the creatures of Nato'wa grow to be. The great majestic animal drew near the hidden ship's remains, and with an air at once disconsolate and lonely, looked here and there as if in search of something or some one long lost and much regretted. Then with a heavy sigh that blew up dust the bear sat slowly down, grotesquely like a man, the picture of complete dejection.

A droning bot-fly lit upon his ear and stung. In sudden rage the grizzly pawed the air, and at his roar other lesser creatures checked every movement. A spike-buck, bedded in a thicket, froze suddenly, cud-chewing stopped. Birds in the trees grew still and even the leaves seemed to whisper in awe when this mightier visitor spoke.

But as the bear stood upright, the lord of all his neighborhood, a dripping mass flew hurtling against his heavy head and struck with a sodden *smack* and streams of golden honey trickled down upon the massive chest.

Taken off balance, the bruin toppled over backward. A jay laughed heartily overhead, but no whit louder than another voice, its owner as yet unseen. At sound of that voice the giant bear rolled lightly to his feet, and with a yelping cry absurd in one so huge and heavy, stood up erect again, and quivering with eagerness peered every way with little red nearsighted eyes.

A moment there was silence. Then came a voice to aid him.

"*Hai*, Aki! Rich yellow honey! Come get thy share. 'Twas worth these little stings to rob that dripping store!"

And now the bear caught sight of a human figure squatting on a lofty limb, with naked back against the rugged trunk. In either hand the figure held great chunks of honeycomb, and on his breast and body the stuff was smeared. Elsewhere upon his bare tanned skin, uncounted flaming marks betrayed the price paid for his loot.

Roaring with delight, great Aki reared beneath the limb and begged with gaping mouth. Down into the open jaws the supple youth flung dripping hunks of comb and honey. Devouring the last morsel, he licked his fingers and drew a muscular forearm across his mouth.

"With smoke Kioga drove the bees away and robbed the hive. *Hai-yah,* but I am full, friend Aki! What better now than to find a sunny ledge and sleep until the hunting-hour?"

And the lithe, smooth-skinned Kioga dropped to earth as lightly as a tree leaf falls. The bear fell to all fours. Then began the scene which ever marked each fresh reunion of this strange, almost inseparable pair. They tumbled, wrestled, rolled upon the ground. The bear struck mighty blows that never fell. The boy dodged in and out, pulling Aki's ears and seeking with his lesser strength to pin that mighty friendly adversary to the earth. The round young muscles writhed and swelled beneath his naked skin, and when huge Aki flicked a paw and caught him unawares, Kioga tumbled through the forest trash which stuck to him wherever the honey had spread.

Upon a ledge not far away a sinuous striped form crouched, whining at the sight of that young and tender prey he dared not spring upon while Aki stood near by. From high afar, eyes like yellow corn burned fires of hate upon Kioga. Of those eyes were seven pairs belonging to T'yone and his ravening pack, who, had they numbered a few more, might even now have dared give chase to Kioga, human consort of the bears of Indegara.

Presently the game of rough-and-tumble ended, and they who had made that glade a bedlam melted out of view, leaving only silence. Of those who watched, but one dared even follow Guna of the hundred stripes. But Guna had not taken ten long padding steps when, from a limb, a lithe form swung to ground, grimaced defiantly, and before the tiger could gather up his wits, sprang quickly out of reach again, returning shrill jeer for throaty roar. Thus did Kioga mock the Enemy of Men, until Aki loomed dark upon the scene, and Guna turned away.

Kioga and Aki turned toward a certain steaming pool upon a mountain-side. There, in the waters of a sulphur spring, Kioga bathed and washed the sticky honey from his skin and hair, then, with Aki likewise dripping at his side, turned toward the coast again. . . .

Upon a rock that overlooked the foamy chaos of the inner reefs, Kioga mourned the fickleness of men—the savage red-skinned Shoni men with whom, until not long ago, he had made his home, almost as much an Indian as they themselves.

"*Ho*, faithful Aki, glad am I that you are not a man. For men are friends today and foes tomorrow. 'Twas only recently that all Hopeka hailed Kioga, who brought them warning of the flood which swallowed up the old Hopeka-town. They brought me juicy meats and sweets to eat. *Ahai* . . . . but that was moons ago, when friends outnumbered foes. Hopeka's walls are rising up again. But now I am not welcome there—and know you why, my mighty friend?"

Great Aki twitched his heavy ears attentively.

"Because I was adopted of Mokuyi and Awena, who treated me as if I were their son. The Long Knives slew them, Aki—in dead of night they crept upon them, killed them in the dark, even as in the long ago they slew my white-skinned parents. And why? Because they knew too much. All four knew that the Long Knives sought to kill wise old Sawamic, emperor-chief of all the Shoni tribes."

Kioga paused, his eyes dark with the recollection of those recent tragedies. The hand with which he worried Aki's ear was quivering, but not with fear. "I caught them in the act, and now they would kill me as well, because I put Sawamic on his guard. And know you, Aki, what the Shoni law commands? Listen:

"Whoso kills thy father or thy mother, him thou must then destroy, and all his blood and issue, until not one remains. Whoso breaks this law shall bear the name of coward, and go about with hanging head, and wear a woman's garments."

"So speaks the Shoni law—and look you, Aki, the Long Knives have slain both those who took me in, and those who gave me life—four lives I must avenge, or bear the name of coward, I, the

Snow Hawk, who laugh right into Guna's very teeth!"

Kioga's voice had risen in intensity. The great bear growled in sympathy as Kioga fell silent, staring moodily at the crags below. For the white boy's intelligence was keen; what reprisal upon his enemies would bring back to him his beloved dead?

Still brooding, his staring eyes were suddenly caught by a bit of time-bleached cordage caught in a cleft at his feet—white man's rope like that shown him by Mokuyi long ago among the few relics of his white parents. Some nesting bird—the *Cherokee*? At once Kioga sprang to his feet and took up again a quest he had maintained for years—the search for the wrecked vessel that had brought his white parents hither. Must it not be somewhere near this spot?

"Men of my race have mighty lodges," Kioga continued on a theme that never lost its fascination for his semi-savage mind. "Lodges that go higher than the lightest arrow flies. Pale-skins tame the cataracts, and make the lightning work for them."

Thus for a little time Kioga rambled vaunting on as once again he searched the shore for traces of his father's ship.

Elsewhere, not far away, three sinewy human figures passed like silent apparitions through the forest. Each was painted on breast and face in figures of red and blue—insignia of the Long Knife secret brotherhood, a rebellious malcontent society among the Shoni tribal federation. All three were naked but for moccasins and for breech-cloth belted round the waist. In every belt a knife and tomahawk was thrust. Keen arrows and strong hunting bows completed their savage armament.

They did not speak, except by silent hand-signs, and every eye was on a fresh-made trail—the spoor left by Kioga. Then suddenly one of the trailing party pointed, hissing, to a tear upon a limb whence branch had been ripped away. From time to time, along Kioga's trail, they found the chips of his whittling. The last of these still showed the damp of recent cutting.

The painted apparitions trod more swiftly yet, and with redoubled caution, and presently they glimpsed a well-known and much-hated figure seated on a rock within short arrow-range. Each looked to each, with eyes that glittered like the snake's as it writhes toward its prey.

Then, as by prearrangement, they separated and stole apart, until each one commanded a different shooting-angle. Here was no sporting chance for the unlucky prey, but a three-fold stacking of the cards of chance, that Kioga might not escape their arrows.

Now slowly to one knee the nearest warrior rose and nocked an arrow to his bowstring. He drew the weapon to an arc, sighting down the shaft with extra care, at little more than point-blank range. Then with a vibrant *twang* the bow released its deadly missile. The shaft sped like a flash of light. Kioga dropped as one pole-axed. Two of the warriors saw him fall.

The third saw nothing, nor ever would again. No will of his had loosed that pointed death. A sudden unexpected blow, delivered by the mightiest thews in all the forest, had fallen on him, crushing the skull. The armored paw of Aki dripped with blood. He crouched above the prostrate warrior, watching for a sign of life, in order to crush it out.

The killing was a silent one among the thickets. The other warriors suspected nothing, but seeing Kioga fall, sprang from concealment, threw aside their bows, and with knives drawn raced in from either side, to count first *coup* upon Kioga, and bear his scalp away in triumph.

They blundered there. The nearest came within ten feet before he realized his error.

Upon his side Kioga lay, indeed. But in his hand the bow was arched, an arrow on the cord, green eyes ablaze behind its feathers. In a limb beyond him was the arrow of the dead would-be assassin.

The startled warrior yelled and wildly flung his knife. With greater coolness Kioga simultaneously loosed his whizzing shaft, impaling the foe with a true heart shot that brought him down in middle stride. The thrown blade passed high above Kioga's head, toward the one remaining Long Knife warrior.

Dodging the flying blade, the enemy drew back his tomahawk to throw, then beheld a shaggy juggernaut charging upon him. From startled haste, his cast was over-quick. The war-ax struck the great bear flatly, but adding to the fury of his charge. The red man turned and fled, with Aki in full chase.

Kioga's haste to drop at first sound of plucked bowstring had saved his life. His heart beat fast with keen excitement. But not the slightest tremor shook his steady hand as Aki returned, the chase abandoned.

"There is to be no peace. Here lie the proofs!" Kioga turned the nearer body with his toe. "This one is Little Wolf, one of the Long Knife secret brotherhood. And this one,"—proceeding to the spot where Aki had got in his lethal stroke,—"no paint could hide the greatest part of Big Nose. Had I but half thy strength, my Aki, they had not dared to hunt me down. Three came and two are dead. One then is left, Thirty Wounds. He is a coward. He'll trouble us no more."

(But there Kioga presumed upon good fortune. The enemy beat a swift retreat, but only to the summit of a ridge nearby. There, glancing back, he glimpsed Kioga and the giant bear departing by another trail. With caution now redoubled, the sinewy savage again pursued.)

Kioga's eyes roved from foe to fallen foe. Gone was the happy, carefree smile, and in its place upon that youthful face strange bitter marks, contrasting darkly with the clear and shining eyes.

He spoke to shaggy Aki in soft low tones, pitched at a grimmer level. His voice seemed older than his years:

"Many moons have passed since the Long Knives slew Awena and Mokuyi in their sleep. Many moons since I took sacred vow of vengeance on the guilty ones. I broke my vow. I walked the peaceful trail. For this the red men's gods are angry with me. This is their first warning—but they will strike again."

He passed a strong hand through his tangled hair, in a gesture of weariness and uncertainty. "*Ai-ya*, blood must flow to satisfy the Shoni gods. Big Nose and Little Wolf are the last of their clan, and they are dead. But there remain Thirty Wounds and his two children and a woman. And when I think of that, my blood grows thin as water."

The Snow Hawk spoke those last words heavily. "If I do not take their lives the spirits of Mokuyi and Awena will never rest," the Indian in him muttered, and thus for a while he sat in deep and troubled thought. His face grew set in harder lines; presently he spoke again:

"My heart is flint. What does Kioga owe the kin of Thirty Wounds? Did they not throw the stones that drove me often from the village? Have I not lived a wolf because they hated my white skin and drove me out to dwell among the forest beasts?" He threw back his shoulders defiantly. "Come, Aki—let us seek them out and have an end!"

And with the words Kioga rose and turned toward Hopeka-town where dwelt the family of Thirty Wounds.

But words alone do not achieve a resolution. In half a mile he turned ten times. He kicked a stone and limped more slowly, though it did not pain him. Although he was not tired, he paused to rest upon a rotting log. Beside him Aki followed suit, and then suddenly, what with that enormous extra weight, their seat gave way and both fell through into a dark and musty place, damp with the smell of long decay. It was a quick and sudden fall, and in the thickets out along their back-trail, a pair of dark eyes narrowed at their startling disappearance. A painted form inched forward through the brush with utmost stealth.

Twisting in mid-air, Kioga alighted on his feet, while Aki fell more heavily, and as their eyes accommodated to the darkness, both looked round about them in amazement.

They crouched within a gloomy chamber, lighted chiefly from the hole above, which they had caused, but with a glow diffusing also through a round hole on one side. A moment Kioga's glance leaped here and there. Then in husky vibrant tones, more full of awe than any outcry could be, he spoke his wonder:

"The ship! The *Cherokee!* My father's ship is found at last!"

All his short life Kioga's dreams had bubbled with imaginary pictures of his father's homeland and the countless wonders there of which Mokuyi oft had spoken. Now here he stood upon the threshold of a greater knowledge of that far exterior world. He felt his blood leap quick with high anticipation.

A moment more, the while he tamed his leaping heart to this magnificent discovery. Then with a careful step he moved about what was, in fact, the cabin of a little vessel that had been covered by shifting sand and driftwood. In the semi-darkness, in a bracket, a ship's lamp hung. He touched it gingerly, not knowing what it was, and in the handling broke the glass. He turned a little screw. Wonder of wonders, up rose a little blackened wick, that had a peculiar smell! He also heard the gurgle of a fluid, but could not judge the uses of this curious thing.

Examining the wick, he knew the black for char. That suggested a wick, for the Shoni used a sort of tallow dip; and making fire with his fire-stick, he held it to the wick, which sputtered up. The sickly flame rose weirdly, lighting up the strange interior.

Ahead he dimly saw a half-open door. Approaching cautiously he passed through into the bow of the *Cherokee.* Forward the little vessel was a wreck. The chain-locker, burst open, contained but a short remaining length of rusted links, which clanked at his touch. Her bow timbers were all stove in. This must have been her mortal wound, received on that frightful passage through the southern reefs.

The galley too was in ruins, but of its fittings Kioga salvaged some old pots and an iron frying-pan, bearing them into the main cabin aft. There things were in better case. The well-built hardwood deck had kept out wet and weather. Breathless with eagerness, Kioga pursued his discoveries, with mighty Aki looking on and digging on his own account for little creatures that had made the rotting ship their home.

A heavy chest was first to catch Kioga's eye, bound round with metal bands, and by some cunning mechanism locked beyond his immediate powers to open it. For half an hour Kioga tugged and pried and tore his nails in his efforts to uncover what must be contained within. His labors went for naught. Defeated, he looked about elsewhere.

In one dark corner lay a wooden box, held together by a snap-clasp which presently sprang open at his fingers' experimental pressure. The cover fell away. Out upon the floor there clattered several objects the like of which he had never seen before.

One was a thing of rusted metal, with a wooden grip at its broad end, and narrowing toward the other, with on one edge a row of countless teeth. Squatting on a bench, Kioga took it up in wonder and chanced to let it scrape along his wooden seat. The teeth removed some bits of wood and left a scar. He repeated the action. The scar grew deeper. He did it yet again. A little heap of wood-dust piled up on the floor as he continued it. He found a certain rhythm in the rasping, back and forward movement. Then, all in an instant he glimpsed the vast utility of this, to him, extraordinary thing—a common carpenter's saw.

Delighted with the deepening cut it made, he sawed like mad. Soon there came the crackle of breaking wood, and down Kioga sprawled upon the floor, the bench on which he knelt sawn through.

Kioga looked from saw to chest, a great idea dawning. He laid the teeth against the wooden cover and sawed away until he heard a harsh and grating sound—steel teeth on metal lining. The saw would cut no deeper. Foiled once again Kioga turned back to the box of tools. But now his quick intelligence suggested what before he had not understood. These several objects had a definite use. With patience he would discover what and why they were.

He took a piece of wood up in his hand. Sunk in it was a little glass, containing viscous fluid. A little bubble moved back and forth as Kioga shifted the angle of the stick. It was an ordinary level, but confounded him completely.

But here was something more engaging. A round and flattened handle, with a curving grip below it, and in a kind of jaw a bit of oddly twisted pointed metal. He took it up. A point suggested a hole. He pressed it against the table, bore down without result until, by accident, he turned the curving handle, and saw the bit twist deep into the cabin table. He caught on instantly, and as he bored the steel went through the wood as if it were but wax, leaving a clean round hole.

Thus, little by little, Kioga discovered a few of the manifold uses of the tools found in the tool-box. One cut; another bored holes. Alone no tool was capable of very much, but wielded together, by a skillful hand, they could accomplish mighty works. Thus, in the semi-darkness of that little wrecked ship's cabin, Kioga vaguely recognized the uses of those implements by which the people of his race had raised themselves above the level of their forbears.

Ere now his own cunning hands had fashioned naught but arrow-points, spearheads and knives of flint or bone, the weaponry of war and hunting—destructive things the which he needed in his perilous forest life. He had been moving toward a life of barbarism, which must destroy in order to survive, with a like destruction lurking always in his path.

But now a nobler vision rose before him. With these new implements, a builder—a creator—he would learn to be, and bring a new advancement to his savage people. He dreamed great dreams of how his skill and craft would lighten the rebuilding of Hopeka's palisade and make the rude Shoni lodges more livable and lasting.

Once more he would be welcome among the red men, as moons ago when his warning had saved a thousand tribesmen from the roaring waters of Metinga Lake. Hopeka-town and all the Shoni folk must surely hail him who redeemed them from the labors of their savage life, and taught them the magic uses of these wonderful new tools!

Now and in the days that followed, he would practice with these tools and learn their every possibility. But first he would go back to the locked chest. He tried with each new tool he found, to open it. Each trial was vain. Behind him, as he worked, the shadow of a head rose up outside the porthole. A face streaked with lines of green and yellow pigment appeared. Gleaming eyes roved the cabin, a strange mixture of wonder and cunning in their expression.

Intent upon his discoveries, Kioga did not notice.

Upon a hook beside the door he found a rusty ring, with other rusty little objects fastened to it which rattled musically when he shook it—a bunch of keys—another baffler. For these he could conceive no use, and idly swinging them on one forefinger, he crouched intently before the chest again, as if by scowling at it he could make it fly apart and reveal its alluring secrets.

He concentrated on the giant padlock once again. And now there awoke in his mind recollection of tales Mokuyi had told him—tales of the white man's life, its creation to barter and exchange, its strange money which was always guarded by lock and key. He looked again at the rattly objects on the metal ring. One of them seemed to fit the hole within the padlock perfectly. He fumbled about, gave a twist and felt the thing of metal grate and turn within the mechanism. He heard a sudden *click,* and at the sound the lock flew sharply open.

With quivering fingers Kioga drew the padlock from the eye-bolt, raised up the iron hasp, and then, with gleaming eyes, threw wide the cover of the chest, while Aki peered over his shoulder.

This was the chest in which the Snow Hawk's white-skinned surgeon father had stored articles intended to be traded with the Alaskan Indians, on whom he hoped to bestow his medical skill and white man's learning. Such things as met Kioga's eager gaze within!

The chest was filled with bolts of bright red cloth and children's toys and trinkets of a hundred kinds—so many that Kioga scarce knew which to take up first; and everything in perfect order and condition, thanks to the sound construction of the chest.

Here was a roundish box, alluring because it had a cover screwed down on it, concealing the contents. A moment while he puzzled out the secret of the turning top. Then slowly he unscrewed it, pausing to prolong suspense and wonder what was in it, while Aki sniffed it with a comic caution.

All at once the top flew off. A long and yellow thing, shaped like a snake, sprang into air. Both Aki and Kioga staggered backward in surprise. Some moments passed before either dared to touch that strange toy with the spring concealed inside of it. Thereafter Aki kept his distance from the chest, regarding it with vast suspicion from the farthest corner.

The ship was growing cold. Kioga built a small hot fire in a big pan to break the chill. Rummaging further among the contents of the chest, he found another box with bright brass fittings on its either end. This too he sought to draw apart, when, as he pulled, discordant strains of music magically issued forth, to startle them. It was a child's accordion; as Kioga worked the various keys, the tunes would change; and for a time this held Kioga charmed, and Aki too forgot his suspicion.

Then something else came into view, some small and red-wrapped packages, marked *"Made in China."* On one the wrappings had torn, exposing a double row of small red paper cylinders. From each of these a short white tail protruded, and all the slender tails were braided into one. Kioga knocked the package on the floor, and Aki, in a playful mood, flipped it into the air.

The packet fell close to the fire. About to bat it round the cabin, Aki snorted in surprise. A little thread of sparks and pungent yellow smoke was spitting from one of these slender tails!

Then happened that which set their nerves on edge—a sputter and *pop-pop-pop*, as with a wondrous crackling din the bunch of firecrackers exploded, dancing all about the cabin floor, and settling finally into a little smoking heap.

Flattened back against the wall, Aki and Kioga stared at it in profound amazement, and seeing that nothing happened, they presently dared approach it. With a stick Kioga stirred the smoking heap and watched to see results. Still nothing happened. He circled it as cat would circle mouse, and touched it from the other side.

Also grown bolder, Aki pushed it with a stealthy claw. Nothing happened even now. He dared to take one sniff, most gingerly, each mighty muscle on the stretch. His breath blew up the sparks. Then swiftly, with a sharp resounding *crack!* the last live firecracker burst and filled his nose with stinging powder-fumes. That was too much for Aki.

Wheeling, catlike, he reared, reached for the hole of entry, and with a frantic scramble, was up and crashing out into the forest, bleating like a two-months' cub. Kioga stood alone among his newfound treasures and laughed until his sides ached.

And now several lockers on the wall challenged for attention. And now he realized these little keys were his open sesame to them all. But first he whistled Aki near, enticing him back finally to the entry-hole. Nearer than that the great bear would not come, but watched proceedings from above.

Kioga opened the nearest locker with a key. Some rolls of paper—maps or charts—fell upon the floor. He sought to examine them more closely, but it was growing dark, and so he set them aside for later perusal. Once more he reached into the dimness of the locker. A metal object, hard and cold, he now drew forth.

Before one bulging part it had an odd device, within which was a metal tongue, and over that a cylinder containing small compartments from which protruded round leaden tips. He counted five of these.

That this might be a distant cousin of his own light bow and arrow Kioga never dreamed. His finger hooked the little metal tongue. Feeling it yield, he pulled. There was a sharp metallic *snap* as the hammer fell upon an empty cartridge. A startled "Hai!" escaped Kioga. He held a loaded pistol in his hand, and thought it some strange club, with hollow handle.

And yet—most clumsy for a club, he thought. Perhaps it was a pipe. He put the muzzle to his lips experimentally, but found no bowl wherein to stuff tobacco. He toyed with the mechanism of the old revolver. He squinted through the black mouthed barrel. His finger fell upon the hammer which, moving backward, also turned the cylinder.

A deadly loaded cartridge now lay in the firing chamber.

Pleased by that earlier *snap*, Kioga's thumb now hooked the trigger awkwardly, and feeling it yield, he pressed again, fascinated by this curious thing of moving parts, and peering into the barrel, seeking to fathom its utility. The hammer fell. Acrid smoke and fire flamed from the pistol mouth. He heard a deafening explosion, and fire burned the hair above his ear.

Then came another mighty crash. The monstrous bulk of Aki fell from above upon the cabin floor beside him and lay there still and silent.

A cry broke from Kioga. He flung himself upon his shaggy friend and raised the heavy head. It fell back limply. There was an ugly wound that bled profusely. Appalled at this calamity to his wild companion, Kioga crouched there, linking thought to thought, recalling what had happened—the smoke, the flame, the loud report.

A half-suspicion growing, he picked up the still smoking pistol. But now he handled it with special gentleness, particularly careful not to touch the trigger. He noticed now that only three of the round lead-colored tips could be seen in the five visible chambers. Before there had been five. He ascertained that one was in the firing chamber by drawing back the trigger, which made the cylinder turn, showing two empty chambers.

This thing, then, reason told him, was a kind of strange misshapen bow, which threw not arrows, but little heavy pellets, with a deadly force. A word sprang into mind that Mokuyi once had used and not explained. This was a "fire-arm."

He turned to Aki once again. Poor Aki's eyes

were closed. A choking something came up into Kioga's throat. He had killed this loyal forest friend! The world grew dark. For Aki of the valiant heart was dead, slain by one who loved him most. The Snow Hawk's vision blurred—and then cleared magically as one of Aki's thick ears twitched beneath his hand.

A moment more and the great bear struggled up, staggering on his feet, his great head shaking. Then from the wound he clawed the flattened leaden pellet that had stunned him, but could not penetrate the armor-plate of bone about his forehead.

Relieved of anxiety for Aki, the Snow Hawk's thoughts went back to the pistol. Here was an arm wherewith to destroy his foes! That thought renewed what, in the excitement of the day, had been almost forgotten—his duty to avenge his dead. It was an unpleasant recollection.

Trying not to think of it, Kioga looked around. One locker still remained unopened. But it would have to wait.

Thirty Wounds and his family—Kioga's vow, his sacred promise, his fourfold duty to his murdered parents, red-skinned and white! Once more his mobile face reflected the black thoughts behind it.

He stuck his new-found weapon through his belt, and with Aki climbed out into the forest, concealed well the entrance to the *Cherokee* and turned toward Hopeka. Upon a ridge he paused hesitant, however, and looked back toward where the ship was hidden. And thus the burning Arctic stars beheld him on the lofty ridge, now looking toward Hopeka-town and vengeance, now gazing toward the coast whence he had come to wrestle with his complex dual nature. . . .

There it was, that implacable Thirty Wounds caught sight of him unguarded now by wandering Aki; and crawling close behind along a rocky ledge above with infinite stealth, the Long Knife warrior upraised the heavy warrior's club thonged to his wrist.

What it was that warned Kioga, it is impossible to tell. Just in time he leaped aside. Lightning-quick, the thought of his new strange weapon came to him; and lightning-swift his hand snatched the revolver from his belt, pointed it at the out-leaning Thirty Wounds and pressed the trigger.

He missed, of course; but so startled was the primitive savage by the flame and smoke and thunderclap of the weapon that he jumped back heedless of his footing, slipped, lost his balance and plunged downward to carom grotesquely from the sloping cliff and land upon the rocks below.

Two circling buzzards saw, and drifted downward toward the silent body. Kioga watched, a superstition in his mind.

"The forest gods have slain my enemy," he decided. "It is a sign of favor. Surely I may wait awhile before I seek out the family of Thirty Wounds."

Drawn by his mystery of that one unopened locker in the *Cherokee*, Kioga now turned back to the derelict again.

He glanced about suspiciously, thrice circling before he entered by the ragged hole that now gave entrance to the drift-covered cabin. He made a little blaze by which to see, and once again tried the keys. Then with a chisel and a hammer he went to work. An hour before dawn found the strong door hanging by one heavy hinge, the locker gaping open. A curious spell fell on him—a spell as of some vast, important happening impending.

Within he saw a small black metal box. Kioga drew it forth, with careful hand. It had a lock. Upon the ring he found a little key to fit it. He turned the key and felt the cover yield, and raised it. At what he saw he felt a little disappointed.

In one compartment there were papers—a bill of sale which named the *Cherokee,* a ship's clearance-papers, a sea letter certifying to the vessel's American ownership, a list of stores, and some other business documents which Kioga skimmed through. He read slowly but without too much difficulty, for Mokuyi had taught him the language of his fathers.

Then came a little packet of letters, tied with a faded ribbon. He opened it, read one of the letters mailed by his fair-skinned mother to his father, many years before. It began *"Beloved"* and ended with her name and tender sentiments.

Kioga tied the packet up with reverent hands, replacing it among his father's other treasured papers, lifted up the top compartment. Below there was a single paper in a brown worn heavy envelope.

Again that sense of coming things was on him. He drew the paper forth, unfolded it, and gave a sudden start, as if a voice had whispered in that silent cabin. He saw these words in round and graceful script, below the date "January 1st, 1863."

"To my dear son, on his sixteenth birthday."

Kioga's eyes went wide. He seemed to feel a gentle hand upon his shoulder. The next lines leaped from the page:

This is a great day in your life. I saw you yesterday. You were a boy no longer; you had become a man. And to a man I now address these words:

As you go on to great achievement, I have these hopes for you:

That you may ever exert yourself to protect the weak. That you may never strike except in self-defense, or in defense of highest principles, but then deliver clean, hard blows, ignoring every low advantage. That you may ever hold life sacred. That you may never harbor hatred in your heart.

I hope that you may ever know the meaning of true chivalry, which even treats an enemy with honor.

And much, much more I hope for you, which cannot be expressed in words.

I send best wishes and my tenderest love.

> *Your friend and father,*
> *Lincoln Rand.*

Kioga devoured the lines again and yet again. Unconsciously he spoke a word he had never before uttered in English. The word he spoke was "Father!"

The echo floated back to him. Startled by the sound of his own voice, Kioga glanced about him. No one was here except himself. And yet, he was not alone, as when he had earlier entered. Aware of this, yet unafraid, he looked toward every corner and out through the glassy port into the forest.

Far in the past another Lincoln Rand—his own great-grandfather—had penned those words to his growing schoolboy son; little dreaming that the last to bear that name would read them amid the shadows of a virgin forest-land unknown to civilized men. . . .

For long Kioga sat in thought, before once more he climbed back to the lofty ridge. There he took three certain arrows from his quiver, which he had set apart for purposes of vengeance. Across his knee he broke them, one by one—he tossed the pieces from the ridge, then settled down to watch the sun rising upon a new day.

PART VI

The Turn of the Tide

Bones tell the story of newfound Arctic Nato'wa: You find them everywhere, all bare and clean and polished—the carrion birds attend to that. Some are the bones of mighty brutes that roamed Nato'wa's forests not long since—great bears, fierce long-haired tigers of an Arctic breed, lithe climbing cats and other brutes both familiar and strange—the fauna of another age.

Those who seek will also find the bones of men—many of them. Some show the marks of savage fangs, but even more will bear the marks of other hostile men, the crushing fracture of a war-club, the jagged perforation of the tomahawk, the clean-cut puncture of a throwing-spear, with often-times a flinten arrowhead wedged intact, in the bone.

By these signs one may know that in Nato'wa, as elsewhere on this earth, man is man's own worst enemy. And on a cliff which overlooks Nato'wa's inner reefs, there is another grim reminder of man's hostility to man: it is a row of human skulls.

Each one stares blankly toward the sea; each one was placed there by some superstitious savage from the nearer inland river-villages of the Shoni tribe, to pacify the unknown dead.

Along this cliff in mournful caucus each day the black-winged purifiers of the forest gather by the hundreds. Each hour sees the vultures come and go upon their endless quest, to keep the wilderness clean of carrion.

Along this cliff one day a lesser meat-bird perched upon a skull. He eyed it with a sharp appraising glance, then settled back indifferently to preen and sleep in the sun. But H'ka the buzzard had hardly closed his eyes when from a distance, hurtling through the air, another skull came flying. With a mighty *clack* it struck H'ka's grim perch from under him, and bowled a dozen others rattling down the cliffs.

H'ka rose upon beating wings, profane and full of indignation. And from the ledge not far above, three grinning faces looked down upon H'ka's discomfiture: One was a bear's face, sly eyes agleam, white teeth exposed from ear to ear, red tongue lolling heavily. A second was the fierce mask of a cougar, the ears back-laid, only the gleaming canines exposed below a wrinkled lip. And in between these well-armed faces of the forest was another, hickory-brown, equipped with even rows of snow-white teeth. Through them came no bestial snarl, but boyish laughter, spontaneous and clear.

Hopeka-town—inland and still not fully re-palisaded since the flood which had leveled it—boasted many promising future warriors, but none among the village youths was so lithely muscular as he who strode between the cougar and the bear, like them a creature of the forest, full of swift abounding strength.

"*Ha-ho!*" he laughed, and spoke aloud to his savage companions. "Who but Kioga could hurl a skull like that? I knocked the skull from under H'ka at thirty paces. But look you—there is one at sixty!" With outstretched arm Kioga indicated the pale gray mark along the cliffs. "Now see this arrow—round in the head, to stun great birds. This one and twenty more I made in half a morning. 'Twould take the finest fletcher in Hopeka-town five times as long. But there again I am superior. For I have tools—ah, cunning tools, keen-edged and made by men who know great magic. They are my father's race. They live, these white-skinned men, where the sun goes to rest in winter. Of our land Nato'wa they know nothing, or they would come and take it from the Shoni warriors. But watch—the arrow flies!"

He took up his bow and drew the string to jaw, glanced down the shaft and raised his aim for distance. Then—*thrum-m-m*—the bow-cord hummed. The shaft shot forth, flew straight for an instant, then curved and, like steel to magnet drawn, it hit the mark resoundingly.

This time there was no bony *clack*. Instead a dull and telltale thump issued from the skull. Two claw-like bony hands flew up in air, then disappeared.

Kioga gasped. "It was a man! Come Mika, Aki—after me! I know of but one skull among the living Shoni so bare of hair as that!"

Another instant later found Kioga reaching down to grasp the wrist of one who desperately clutched a jutting spur of rock at the cliff's edge.

A moment more, and he lay sprawled upon the rock. The Snow Hawk conned him closely.

"K'yopid, as I thought! *Ai*, his eyes are closed. I've killed him with my bird-bolt. But no—he opens one. Ah, he is dazed, no more. Well for thee, K'yopit my sly friend, I did not use a pointed shaft! Wake up! Awake, my wrinkled hypocrite! How things have changed. Once K'yopit thought to make Kioga his slave. And now,"—with a quick movement the youth slipped a thong about the other's wrists—"now I am the master of a shaman, and a very clever one."

"My head! My head!" The captive's groaning voice came full of pathos through his toothless thin-lipped jaws. One eye, wide open, belied his attitude of unconsciousness. It scanned Kioga with a swift and cunning glance. Then suddenly it glimpsed those other two, and feigning death, K'yopit stiffened out again in terror.

"Come, come, K'yopit!" the Snow Hawk cried impatiently. "Awake! These are my creatures; there is naught to fear. What do you here among the Men-of-Long-Ago?"

K'yopit opened up his eyes again, and taking courage, rose to a squatting position, froglike. "My luck was bad. I brought a skull to place upon the pile," he lisped. "For thus bad luck is often cured."

"Ho, K'yopit, long moons have passed since you sought to steal me for your slave."

"Bear me no ill will for that," the other whined. "An old man am I, in dire need of one to break my wood and bring me food."

"You came from far?" pursued the Snow Hawk, guilelessly.

"On foot from distant Magua. They threw me

from the village bodily. I am an outcast now, without a place to lay my head."

"You wring my heart," the Snow Hawk answered, unimpressed. "But tell me, what did you do to anger them?"

"Eh—er," said K'yopit with a shrewd glance at the youth. "He is no fool, this handsome boy from Hopeka! ... I threw the plum-stones with the warriors. The game went on all night. It came to pass, when morning dawned, that each warrior owed me skins he did not have. They were a sorry sight, without a feather to their names, confounded by my skill!" He cocked a knowing eye on Kioga. "Wouldst care to play awhile?"

The Snow Hawk raised a negative hand hastily. "Not I, thou smiling cheat! But look you, shaman: There is another game that I would play."

"Ah, games! You talk my dialect, my son," the shaman answered eagerly. "What have you in your mind?"

"We both are outcasts—" began Kioga.

In surprise the shaman interrupted:

"An outcast, *you?* Who saved the people of Hopeka from Metinga's flooding waters?"

"Even so. The memories of men are short. And you too, so you said."

"Indeed! Segoya threatened to wear my ears about his neck if I returned to claim my gaming debts."

"Well, then, we both wish to regain grace among the Shoni. What would you give me if I showed you how this might be done?"

K'yopit looked uneasy at this talk of giving, then brightened. "My magic secrets I'll reveal to you," he answered slyly.

"Ah, bah! Come, shaman, I know all those little tricks, and more besides. What will you give—of value?"

K'yopit's face counterfeited injured feelings. But when Kioga calmly ignored it, craft took its place. "The half of fifty skins, which I have hidden near by. What's in your mind, my subtle youth?"

"Come walk with us and see." Kioga rose; the shaman too. But old K'yopit shrank back from the panting jaws of Aki and the cougar Mika.

"Come, come!" cried Kioga. "You are too brave to fear my harmless ones. Shrink not. But if you think to do me any evil, depend upon it, Aki will smell the act beforehand, and rip you open like a water-bag."

"I do thee evil?" whined K'yopit indignantly. "*Ai-i!* I love thee like an only son. But what is it, thou wouldst speak about? Come quickly to the point."

"Each step draws us nearer," said Kioga, probing the thickets near the seashore with his quick keen eyes. "Ah, we are here!" Drawing aside a thorny bush, he revealed a heap of wreckage covered by the forest vines. For as with bones of brutes and men, Nato'wa gives final harborage to cadavers of ships as well, which drift by chance where men would never intentionally sail them. Here lay the ruin of a little single-masted ship, a great hole stove in the decking, toward which the Snow Hawk pointed, ordering: "Enter."

K'yopit obeyed, a little fearfully, for never before had he seen the like of this, to him, vast vessel. Kioga followed, as one to whom the way was most familiar, the two brutes crouching at the exit watchfully. Darkness reigned within, but with his fire-sticks, Kioga kindled light, by which the wrinkled shaman saw the strange interior and looked about, wide-eyed.

"Fear not," Kioga reassured him. "Oft have I hidden here of late, when foes pursued me, since first I found this great canoe. My father came here in it from the land of white-skins."

"A race of white-skins? Bah, that I cannot believe."

"Scoff not. Here is their work. Now look you, K'yopit: we both are outcasts, 'tis agreed. And think of this: Hopeka's broken walls are rising slowly. The warmen are away. You may have heard that the Wa-Kanek scalp-hunters are on the march. Another day or two will find them near Hopeka. Many of our tribesmen will be killed without a wall to fight behind."

"Yes, yes," K'yopit muttered. "But what of that?"

"We'll show them how to raise the wall more quickly; and how to make their weapons in a quarter of the time; and how to make their thin canoes great enough to sail upon the ocean; and how to build their lodges stronger than the strongest winds. Then once again we will be welcome among our people, and men will cheer our names."

"Great talk! Great talk!" K'yopit answered doubtfully. "But how may such things be done?"

"We'll bring them white men's knowledge. We'll bring them *tools*, the like of which the Shoni never knew before, which I have found and learned to use these past weeks near this hulk."

" 'Tools,' " K'yopit rolled the foreign word upon an unaccustomed tongue. "What may *'tools'* be?"

"Tools are the implements with which my race—the white men—have conquered half the world." Then selecting a piece of wood: "Here is a good thick branch. Divide it into two," he said.

K'yopit took it up and thought, then held the wood across the fire, charring the center, scraping away the char and burning it again. Slowly and laboriously he thus set to work to divide the wood in two.

The Snow Hawk smiled superiorly, and reached into a chest, drawing forth a rusty but serviceable saw. In five strokes he achieved what K'yopit would have needed an hour to accomplish.

Narrowed grew the eyes of old K'yopit. "Eh-eh, a strange thing, this! How easily all the palisade logs could be cut."

"Here is another piece, a good spear's length. Could you make it smooth?"

K'yopit looked about him, found a small sharp stone and diligently scraped. But Kioga drew forth a plane and with swift and easy movements, made the square billet round, shaped on a point, hardened it in the fire and hurled it against the half-decayed wooden wall, where it struck and quivered. This was the work of but a few minutes.

"Eh-eh," muttered old K'yopit, more and more impressed. "Smooth as a maiden's skin—in such a little while!"

"*Ai!*" the Snow Hawk answered, throwing light about the dim interior. "And now behold the other things that I have made with white men's tools, and tell me if the Shoni tribes would not give all they own to know my secret."

K'yopit glanced about, and saw boxes with hinged tops, and graceful clubs, and miniature canoes, and paddles long and broadly bladed, all of a finish unknown to the primitive workmen of the Shoni tribes.

"*Ai-yah!*" exclaimed K'yopit. "You're right. For this the Shoni folk would give their all."

"Even so," said Kioga. "Now, then, you shall precede me to the village. Tell Saki of the mighty voice, and she will cry the tidings through the village."

" 'Tis good. I go this very hour," K'yopit answered, by now enthusiastic. Then, on another note: "But how shall *I* win favor—who return with nothing?"

"Thy magic caused these things to be—out of thin air," Kioga explained with a knowing glance. "Thine is the magic power. I am but the wielder of the tools. You understand? And thus we both win honors."

K'yopit cackled shrilly. "I understand, O cunning one! I go to tell them you are coming."

Outcast, and dweller for long among the forest brutes, the Snow Hawk craved the companionship of his human kind. Eager as well to bring enlightenment to his savage adopted people, he trod the forest trails light-footed and with even lighter heart. And when he neared Hopeka, with his tools wrapped in a skin bag, he found the ground had been well prepared: Apprised of something strange to come, the people, robed in furs and feather mantles, assembled near the village gate.

Foremost among them, in positions of advantage, stood several of the tribal shamans, jealous of their own reputations as makers of magic, yet consumed by curiosity.

The Snow Hawk neared, bold on the face of him, yet every nerve alert to fly at need. But though his enemies had not forgot their rancor, it smoldered now inactively, replaced by the burning curiosity of their savage natures. No hand was raised against him when he entered. Instead the shamans made a path, through which he went, his bag of tools in hand, and sat before the silent seated council, among whom squatted old K'yopit.

When all had gathered, Semasi uprose and addressed Kioga:

"He of the fleshless limbs spoke of great benefits to all our people which you would bring—of stronger walls, raised more swiftly than our workers now may raise them. Speak, then, and show your magic to the council. And if it be as great as old K'yopit promised, mayhap the chiefs will honor both of you."

K'yopit rubbed his skinny hands in anticipation. Kioga opened up the bag and laid the tools before him.

"Now bring me logs, and I will show you how they may be cut the quicker, that the walls of Hopeka-town will rise before an enemy arrives."

And when the logs were brought, he cut them swiftly through—as many logs in half an hour as several men could burn through in a day, working the ancient way. Then other tools he showed them. The people watched in fascination, all save the circle of the envious shamans, resentful of the stir that Kioga caused.

"A fraud!" cried one, determined that Kioga

should receive no credit. And others quickly joined their voices in the condemnation.

This much Kioga knew, from long experience: the village folk—those lesser ones remaining while the warriors were absent—dared not deny the statements of the influential shamans. He noted more—the stealthy closing of the ring of shamans round about him, and the fingering of weapons. His quick glance sought K'yopit, found him sneaking through the village gate, his hopes of gaining favor gone glimmering.

Without an instant's hesitation Kioga tossed his bag of tools beyond the wall, left behind what remained, and with a lightning and unexpected bound knocked down the nearest robe-wrapped shaman, swung up atop a ledge and thence, cat-like, upon the towering eastern palisade, the only one erected. A knife chugged sharply just between his clutching hands, and yells behind foretold pursuit. But when it came, Kioga had snatched up his bag of tools and gone.

He heard the din die down behind and slackened his pace, then turned to slip along the river. And presently he saw ahead the withered form of old K'yopit, fleeing as if pursued by devils. The Snow Hawk hailed him. K'yopit only scurried on the faster. But Kioga easily came up with him and seized him by the nape.

"Why do you run? 'Tis I, Kioga. *Ai-i*, you are a fearful one!"

"Fearful?" quavered K'yopit. "Fearful—I? Not so—I ran but to lend thee aid, my son."

"But you ran away from the village."

"Eh, well, no matter," returned K'yopit, with

returning self-possession. "We are safe again. Do not complain. What now?"

"What now—I do not know," Kioga answered thoughtfully, much hurt by the failure of his plans. "We still are outcasts. The Shoni do not want us. What say you, K'yopit, if we go away and never return?"

"A fine idea—but whither?" demanded the practical old trader.

"Beyond the reefs, beyond the southern horizon, to the place where the holy sun goes every winter."

K'yopit sought to hide a shiver. "Eh—not that I am afraid, but—the waters of the sea are cold, and I am not the mighty swimmer I used to be."

"There will not be the need to swim. With these my tools, I'll build a great canoe. White men cause the wind to labor, pushing on a great wing called a sail. And on their ships they have a tail to steer by, like a fish. I'll make my ship as white men do. Then we will sail it out to sea and never-more return among the Shoni, who hate us. When we have gone, they'll wonder what became of us."

"But men have never gone among those mighty waves before." K'yopit added, fearfully: "Hark—we near the cliffs above the sea. Hear how the great waves roar and beat against the rocks! No craft could live out there."

"The craft that I will build will laugh at danger. Come, friend K'yopit, had you rather be burnt by the Shoni at the stake?"

"Burn or drown or feed the belly of a shark, I see no difference. A man is dead, no matter how he dies. I'll go—do anything you say."

"That is well," quoth Kioga, turning back. "But look you, it will cost you dearly."

"How's that—eh-eh?" demanded wary K'yopit, once more the miser of Magua.

"For sail we need a score of fine white skins, all sewn together."

"A score of skins," K'yopit wailed. " 'Tis all I own, my son!"

"What of the skins you promised me, then? What of the skins you won in throwing plum-stones?"

"*Ai*, he never forgets a word," complained K'yopit. "But if I must, I must. But only ten skins will I give."

"So long as they are big, mayhap they'll do. Come, let us go and fetch them."

Perforce, though still unwilling, K'yopit led the way to a cave along the cliffs, and from their hiding-place removed a bale of well-cured skins. From these, with his sharp knife, Kioga next day cut long leather thongs, pierced holes, and with the thongs sewed all the skins together.

" 'Tis not a very handsome sail, but it will do. Come now, and let us get to work. The hardest part still remains."

Then began the fabricating of Kioga's ship. Along the shore the Snow Hawk found the driftwood that he sought, and laboriously fashioned a keel. A sapling, cut and trimmed, would serve for mast. But though he labored until the sweat ran from his pores, the work proceeded slowly. And when some time had passed, Kioga looked doubtfully at a sorry-looking skeleton, the least part of his ship-to-be.

He had the tools which he had found, and not a little acquired skill in their use. Possibly a month would have seen completion of his plans. But time was of the essence, for winter neared: the work did not progress with speed enough; and doddering, misanthropic K'yopit proved more a hindrance than a help, commenting: "Methinks 'twould leak before we reached the nearest reef. We cannot go to sea in that."

"K'yopit, you are right," the Snow Hawk answered with a frown. "Had I not left behind my other tools—but wait, I know a better way. Last night it stormed, and after every storm the sea gives up some driftwood and wreckage. We'll hunt along the shore and see what may be found."

Two days they hunted vainly. But on the third their search was well rewarded. Lying between two rocks in a tidal pool, the relic of a little battered single-masted craft—a whaleboat perhaps— was listing, the water spouting from her open seams. When she had emptied, Kioga set to work. The cracks he caulked with pitch and grass; the larger holes repaired with splints of wood. The deck he found in fairly good repair, but to be safe, he reinforced it from within.

And when the waters rose again and filled the tidal pool, Kioga did a dance upon the rickety deck, and shouted down to old K'yopit: "Behold— it floats! It floats!"

Scarce had the words come from his lips, when the vessel wearily settled under him; and on the shore K'yopit shook his head pessimistically.

"No matter," the Snow Hawk said, immensely encouraged by the momentary triumph. "The next time it will stay afloat. Be cheerful, K'yopit— we will yet leave all our foes behind."

"And sail over the earth's edge to destruction!"

"Ah, bah!" Kioga answered, out of patience altogether. "The earth is round, not flat as you would make it. We're going to America, my father's land. When the Shoni come to look for us, we shall be gone, never to return."

As Kioga had promised, he soon performed. When once again the tide came in, the creaky vessel floated and stayed afloat. With lengths of braided rawhide, Kioga moored it to a rock.

"Now food is what we need—good meat to last us many weeks, and great skins filled with water, that we may not thirst upon our voyage. Do you wait here, K'yopit, while I and Mika hunt a deer. Then you shall cure its meat in smoke while I fetch other things."

The Snow Hawk touched the lithe lean cat upon the head and made a little sound. At once the puma bounded up, quivering in every muscle. The two together started up the cliffs and passed into the forest.

They went not very far before Kioga sniffed the air and said a word; whereat the puma flattened, then slunk through the underbrush, toward a high-crowned stag in view in a ravine. Soon, with a snort, the kingly quarry raised his armored head, beheld the creeping death and sprang away along the forest trail—toward Kioga crouched upon a ledge beneath which the deer must rush in charging from the *cul-de-sac*.

Kioga heard its pounding hoofs, beheld its white-rimmed eyes. Then as it fled below, the Snow Hawk pounced, bright blade agleam. One hand closed around an antler's base. The other fell, the sharp flint piercing deep. Down came the stag, its short race run.

Panting with his efforts, Kioga disemboweled the animal, reserving the liver for snarling Mika, but not immediately tossing the cat its share. Skinning his stag, Kioga wrapped the best parts in the skin, heaved it upon his back and staggering beneath the load, delivered it before K'yopit, who started in surprise. "A kill—so soon?"

"Good meat aplenty. Now to get Mika on our ship. Come, Silver One!"—extending in a hand the puma's share of meat, till now withheld. Eager for the feast, but wary of setting foot upon the ship, at last Mika weakened, leaping gingerly upon the deck. Vast Aki, at the sight of the puma eating, soon followed suit, less fearful of the movement underfoot for having ridden often in Kioga's canoe in cubhood days.

"Now," said the Snow Hawk. "Mayhap the river-traders will wish to give us a basket of acorn-meal. Weapons too, we'll need."

This time he set forth alone, to rearrange the ownership of food and weapons. At the mouth of a narrow rivulet he watched for signs of those who daily ferried food and skins between the several river villages. A great canoe soon came, gunwale-deep with articles of trade and tribute. Unhappily, two convoy craft accompanied it, filled with seven warriors each: some strategy beyond a simple seizure must be employed to gain one of those bursting baskets filled with food. He glimpsed the foremost paddler and knew him and the others for a member of the shaman secret brotherhood who long had persecuted him, and this made him the more eager to discomfit them. A little while he trailed the craft, until the paddlers nosed their canoes inshore to take advantage of the slightly calmer water there.

Their speed grew little swifter for the change. Their full attention was devoted to their work. And on the bank, quick wits made instant capital of the circumstances. Along a supple leafy branch Kioga crept. The convoy-craft inched tortoiselike beneath him. The trade-canoe, in tow, came slowly near.

Kioga eyed a bulging basket near the after thwart, filled, he knew, with acorn-meal. He saw good weapons, laid aside in favor of the paddles. The craft was now beneath him, the sweating paddlers moving upstream. The fourth man passed. Kioga waited, gathering his muscles. The fifth showed a bronzed and gleaming back. *Now!*

Stonelike, Kioga dropped from branch upon canoe, hurled overboard the basket and seized four wooden spears. Then ere the paddlers, glancing back, could comprehend the sudden visitation which all but swamped the canoe, Kioga dived headlong overboard.

He rose beside the floating basket, and buoyed by it, drifted out of danger on the hurrying currents. Upriver, the paddlers dared not diminish their labors lest the eddies dash them and their valuable cargo upon the rocks.

With their threatful imprecations in his ears Kioga reached the shore, took up the spears and baskets, and headed for the coast again. He did not note the quiet dropping of fine grains of acorn-meal behind him as he went.

As Kioga went seacoastward, he thought constantly of the voyage just ahead, the great adventure to the Outer World. His burden seemed to lighten with the anticipation; and when he reached the place of skulls on the cliff above ·the sea, it was as if he walked on air. He had turned to follow down the trail, picking his way between the skulls, when suddenly a flight of whining shafts flew past his ears. An arrow nicked him in the arm; another pierced the basket at his back.

Then from behind, a yell of triumph rose; and wheeling to look back, he saw the figures of the canoe-men approaching on the run. He dropped the basket, conscious now of what had happened, a trickle of white meal still coming from the basket, telling its own tale.

The weapons he bore were bound with a thong. He reached for a stone with which to check the rush of his pursuers. His hand fell on a skull. He picked it up and hurled. Straight and true it soared, and bounded from the head of Tamako, who tottered back. Then like a flash Kioga hurled another, and others still, as fast as ever he could throw.

The superstitious red men drew back in horror as the grisly missiles fell among them. And picking up his bundle of weapons Kioga dropped swiftly down the ledges, agile as a leopard, to the shore.

Running now at greyhound speed, the Snow Hawk glimpsed K'yopit on their ship, quivering with fear. "The rope—throw off the rope!" Kioga cried; and sensing his intent, the shaman hastily obeyed. The little craft floated free. Kioga flung the weaponry aboard and leaped after it.

Like lightning now he hauled the ropes to raise the clumsy hide sail. The thin mast creaked, but up the awkward contraption rose. The wind was off the shore and filled it slowly. The boom swung out; the ship began to lean and cut the water.

Ashore, the Indians were checked at the waterline, deterred by one whose tall black dorsal fin curved lazily across the tidal pool. Their arching arrows fell just short of the receding vessel, and K'yopit shrilled a high cracked jeer. At the sound, a thrill rippled up Kioga's spine. The dreamed-of voyage to the Outer World was now begun!

Mist hid the shore. Kioga seized the tiller. Forward, Aki glowered toward the sea. Mika paced the deck aft restlessly. K'yopit stared down overside, shrank back, then stared again. Presently the Snow Hawk saw the reason:

Six long black streamlined forms accompanied them toward the south—wolves of the deep: great orca, bloodthirsty pirates of the teeming Nato'wan waters, who attack the kill the greatest of the sea's leviathans.

"Eh-eh!" the trader quavered, trembling as with ague, and green about the lips and ears. "Not that I am afraid, but—*e-yah*, I like not the looks of these who go with us! Perhaps it would be better if we turn and go ashore again."

"Ashore!" exclaimed Kioga. "I know not even where it lies. The mists grow thick. 'Twere better that you go below. No good will come of telling them you fear them."

Glad to desert his place, K'yopit shuffled out of sight, leaving the Snow Hawk to struggle alone with unforeseen problems of simple navigation. For when he put his helm hard over, in steering round a dangerous rock, the wind seized strongly on his heavy sail and heeled the small ship over on a second course, ofttimes more perilous than the first. And as the boom swung back and forth, he must dodge it constantly.

In spite of this, the little craft made headway

from the land, though more than once the jagged rocks ground harshly on her barnacled hull. By now the offshore wind blew much more strongly. Kioga's sail was bulging, full of it. The sapling mast creaked in its fittings. Close astern, a white wake bubbled loudly, and in the taut-drawn cordage the wind made wild deep-humming music.

The Snow Hawk yelled for joy. "Tomorrow we will reach America, my father's land," he told the tiller-arm, ignorance his buckler against all doubt.

As if in answer to his voice, one of the orca breached to blow, and sprayed the deck with salty foam. And then, without the slightest warning, a rope let go. The sail flagged forward. The mast bent, buckled near the deck, then dropped into the sea.

With headway lost, the craft yawed, rocking at the mercy of the waves, which showed no mercy but beat down heavily against the shaky craft. A scarf of milky foam boiled up above the forward rail. A long green sea next raked the little pitching ship from end to end. Great Aki wrapped both mighty arms about the mast-stump and clung. Mika, snarling like a grinding mill, crouched low, bedraggled by the flying spume.

Wrestling with the tiller, now gone wild, Kioga thought of poor K'yopit, huddled fearfully below, when suddenly the trader's long hairless head appeared above the deck. And instead of fear Kioga saw, with quick surprise, a changed K'yopit: The trembling gait was gone. The wind-blown white crest of a wave slapped the old fellow to his knees, but he rose, undaunted and shouted out defiantly the semblance of a war-cry.

"*Hai-yah!* Do not turn back—sail on!"

"I would," Kioga answered, "but that the mast has fallen."

"Ah, bah! 'Tis nothing!" K'yopit wheezed impatiently; and when an orca rose again to blow, he seized a spear and hurled it with the vigor of a man of thirty. When the spear struck true, he danced triumphantly. "Sail on!"

"What happened you?" Kioga cried.

"I am a match for any man, ten men—*ehi*, for twenty!" K'yopit shouted, pounding on his bony wizened chest.

"Then use your strength. Here is a spear. A moment more, and we'll be on the rocks. Push hard, K'yopit, if you'd live to see the white man's country!"

K'yopit did as bidden. And as he grasped the spear, a round and shiny object fell from underneath his tattered robe, and crashed to fragments on the deck. A brownish liquid trickled from the pieces.

"What's that?" Kioga called, above the roaring of the waves. "It has a mighty smell."

"I found it down below and drank it almost empty. With every gulp I felt a younger man. There are a score again as many in a chest."

"Push hard!" Kioga yelled. "Too late!" he added as a great wave lifted the ship and dropped it heavily upon a ledge of rock. "We are aground. The tide moves out. We must remain until it comes in again and floats us free."

"Fear not," K'yopit shrilled in words that fell upon each other. "Come below with me, and drink of the magic water."

Kioga eyed the aged trader sharply. "His eyes are red. His face is flushed. He stutters," he muttered softly to Aki. "White men make potent medicines. Mayhap K'yopit found them."

The Snow Hawk took stock of their situation: The vessel was jammed fast on a sloping ledge. Naught but some outside force could ever set it free. He glimpsed the mighty grizzly climbing off upon the reef. The answer struck him.

"Aki, thy great strength shall help us. I'll tie these ropes round thy shoulders, thus—and fasten the other ends upon the sides of the ship—so. Now, then, K'yopit, since you have such strength, come help us."

K'yopit came, all confidence, flattered by the words, and obeyed. Kioga pushed against great Aki, and Aki gave a mighty lunge. What with the efforts of all three, the craft leaned over. A moment more, and it had been afloat. But all this stress and strain had proved too much for the rickety vessel. It creaked and groaned, then fell apart in separate pieces, which instantly were swamped.

"We are marooned. Our food is lost, our boat a wreck," Kioga declared, picking himself up from where the rope had dragged him. "*They* know it too," he added somberly, watching their companions of the outward voyage lifting ugly snouts above the water in the distance. Defiantly he shook his fist.

"Think not that you will dine on us, O blubber flukes! Blow, vultures of the sea. Gnash, hungry ones! Whales thou mayst kill, and helpless seals; but we will prove thy match, although in numbers thou hast grown to twelve!"

"Come, Aki, Mika! Stand up, K'yopit—is it cowardice that makes thee stagger back?"

"I? Afraid?" K'yopit answered thickly, dully indignant. "Lead on. We four will stand against the powers even of the sea!"

The four waited there upon the reef until the tide was well out, and the reefs and ridges over which they had sailed this far gleamed bare and wet, with here and there great lakes and pools which never did recede. The four set out to get back to the mainland, quitting their lofty place of wreckage, and filing down into the valleys of the reefs, now seldom more than knee-deep in water.

Upon a peak beyond Kioga paused after some hours, to look back southward toward the misted sea and the vanishing wreck of his little ship, which should have carried him to far adventure in his father's land. His shoulders slumped a little, and for all that he was now nearly seventeen, a slight quiver of the lip betrayed his deep regret.

From far behind, the faintest whisper for a moment, he heard a quiet mutter. He knew it for the returning tide, which sweeps in upon Nato'wa's coast with a power and a fury known nowhere else upon the earth.

"Quick!" cried the Snow Hawk, starting off. "The waters of the sea are coming. Make haste!"

K'yopit followed; and close on their heels came limping Mika and the bear, each footprint bloody. But now they had a constant reminder in that mounting roar behind them, more sinister for the fog which gave no glimpse of danger, while greatly amplifying sounds of it.

"I cannot walk longer," K'yopit cried at last, stumbling. "Do you go on alone."

"His courage holds," thought Kioga, but to the

other said: "Hold to my shoulders—make haste, I'll help you."

Thus for a little time they made fair speed. But now the waters shouted behind. The fog lifted. Glancing back above one shoulder, Kioga saw what is called the primary crest—that first inflow of foam and small débris, spurred on by that fierce sea-squall cracking its whip of wind behind.

He held K'yopit tighter, set his teeth and struggled on, encouraged by a glimpse of land, and Mika climbing wearily up to safety among the rocks. Close by, faithful Aki rolled limping toward the land.

Kioga seized him by the scruff. "On, Aki," he whispered. The huge brute surged forward. The waters of the primary crest were at their heels, now swirling round about their ankles, their knees, their thighs. A moment more, and Aki was afloat, and swimming more swiftly than he could have run on those poor bleeding feet, with a youth and an aged man clinging to him for dear life.

Now in their ears the sea was bellowing. A look back revealed a sight that almost stopped Kioga's heart: the curving main tide-crest, uprearing like some stupendous animal tossing a snowy mane of yellow spume. K'yopit shrieked in terror. Even Aki's roar was shrill with fear. Kioga clenched his jaws, white-lipped.

Then with a crash like stunning thunder the tidal crest smote full against the sloping cliffs. Kioga's grip on Aki broke. The aged shaman was torn from his grasp. Smothered in foam, he saw black rocks before his eyes, reached, caught hold, hit hard against the cliffs, the breath gone from his body, where he lay wedged between the rocks.

Unconscious for a moment, Kioga awoke to hear men's cries, almost lost in the roaring of the sea. He saw K'yopit seized by lean brown hands. He saw a warrior bend above himself. This was to be the end—of him who until now had defied the best of them! Strengthless, Kioga waited for the killing stroke with open eyes, a stoic to the last.

But to his surprise, the warriors gathered round about him, then raised him up and bore him on their shoulders toward the forest. He saw Miloka, once his father's friend, among them.

"Mock not my helplessness," Kioga said. "For if I am to die, I wish to die with proper dignity, like a warrior."

Miloka laughed aloud. "He talks of death, this Snow Hawk! He talks of death, who showed our people how to raise their walls so swiftly that when the Wa-Kanek came we laughed into their faces, and blotted them from our forests. Death—*ai!* But death to them who sought to kill thee, Kioga. Tonight we feast thee and thy wrinkled friend."

"Didst hear, K'yopit?" cried Kioga.

"Eh-eh," answered K'yopit between coughs which racked him still; "I heard, but when I think of those flagons sinking in our ship! Now shall I always remain a coward, as I was before."

But Kioga did not hear him. He heard instead a strange wild scream—the cry of Mika, in the distance. And back upon the cliffs, a bear's vast and shaggy form sat looking after their departure.

"You'll be a chief, before too long," Miloka now was saying. But even this Kioga did not hear. For what he long had sought—reunion with the Shoni tribesmen, high honors in the tribe—was far from mind.

His thoughts were with a little broken ship far out beyond the inner reefs.

Lin Carter's bestselling series!

☐ **UNDER THE GREEN STAR.** A marvel adventure in the grand tradition of Burroughs and Merritt. Book I.
(#UY1185—$1.25)

☐ **WHEN THE GREEN STAR CALLS.** Beyond Mars shines the beacon of exotic adventure. Book II. (#UY1267—$1.25)

☐ **BY THE LIGHT OF THE GREEN STAR.** Lost amid the giant trees, nothing daunted his search for his princess and her crown. Book III.
(#UY1268—$1.25)

☐ **AS THE GREEN STAR RISES.** Adrift on the uncharted sea of a nameless world, hope still burned bright. Book IV.
(#UY1156—$1.25)

☐ **IN THE GREEN STAR'S GLOW.** The grand climax of an adventure amid monsters and marvels of a far-off world. Book V.
(#UY1216—$1.25)

DAW BOOKS are represented by the publishers of Signet and Mentor Books, **THE NEW AMERICAN LIBRARY, INC.**

ALAN BURT AKERS—the first five great novels of Dray Prescot is The Delian Cycle:

☐ **TRANSIT TO SCORPIO.** The thrilling saga of Prescot of Antares among the wizards and nomads of Kregen. Book I. (#UY1169—$1.25)

☐ **THE SUNS OF SCORPIO.** Among the colossus-builders and sea raiders of Kregen. Book II. (#UY1191—$1.25)

☐ **WARRIOR OF SCORPIO.** Across the forbidden lands and the cities of madmen and fierce beasts. Book III. (#UY1212—$1.25)

☐ **SWORDSHIPS OF SCORPIO.** Prescot allies himself with a pirate queen to rescue Vallia's traditional foes! Book IV. (#UY1231—$1.25)

☐ **PRINCE OF SCORPIO.** Outlaw or crown prince—which was to be the fate of Prescot in the Empire of Vallia? Book V. (#UY1251—$1.25)

DAW BOOKS are represented by the publishers of Signet and Mentor Books, THE NEW AMERICAN LIBRARY, INC.

ALAN BURT AKERS

Six terrific novels compose the second great series
of adventure of Dray Prescot: The Havilfar Cycle.

☐ **MANHOUNDS OF ANTARES.** Dray Prescot on the unknown continent of Havilfar seeks the secret of the air-
boats. Book VI.   (#UY1124—$1.25)

☐ **ARENA OF ANTARES.** Prescot confronts strange beasts
and fiercer men on that enemy continent. Book VII.
                                   (#UY1145—$1.25)

☐ **FLIERS OF ANTARES.** In the very heart of his enemies,
Prescot roots out the secrets of flying. Book VIII.
                                   (#UY1165—$1.25)

☐ **BLADESMAN OF ANTARES.** King or slave? Savior or be-
trayer? Prescot confronts his choices. Book IX.
                                   (#UY1188—$1.25)

☐ **AVENGER OF ANTARES.** Prescot must fight for his enemies in order to save his friends! Book X.
                                   (#UY1208—$1.25)

☐ **ARMADA OF ANTARES.** All the force of two continents
mass for the final showdown with Havilfar's ambitious
queen. Book XI.   (#UY1227—$1.25)

DAW BOOKS are represented by the publishers of Signet
and Mentor Books, THE NEW AMERICAN LIBRARY, INC.

THE NEW AMERICAN LIBRARY, INC.,
P.O. Box 999, Bergenfield, New Jersey 07621

Please send me the DAW BOOKS I have checked above. I am enclosing
$_____(check or money order—no currency or C.O.D.'s).
Please include the list price plus 35¢ a copy to cover mailing costs.

Name_____

Address_____

City_____ State_____ Zip Code_____
Please allow at least 4 weeks for delivery